CONTENTS

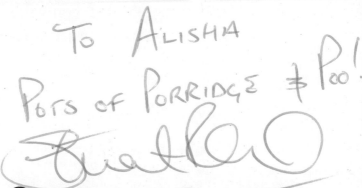

To Alisha
Pots of Porridge & Poo!

Gorgeous George

And the Unidentified, Unsinkable Underpants

Part 01

By

Stuart Reid

Illustrations, Cover and Layouts
By John Pender

Gorgeous Garage Publishing Ltd
Falkirk, Scotland

Cover design and illustrations by John Pender
Cover and illustrations copyright © Gorgeous Garage Publishing Ltd

Photographs used by kind permission
of Jess Reid and John Pender

Second Edition
This edition published in the UK by
Gorgeous Garage Publishing Ltd
ISBN 978-1-910614-07-5

www.stuart-reid.com

DEDICATION
Thanks to John.

Reading Rocks!

*For my wife Angela and my little boy Lucas.
Who's love, encouragement and unrelenting
patience means the absolute world me.*

*Thank you for letting daddy
live out his drawing dream!*

*Love always,
John xXx*

(And Stuart... you're very welcome!)

Prologue

The earth shifted. Not much but enough.

No one noticed, at first. It wasn't an earthquake or even a tremor, just an underground rumbling like the giant belly of a hungry beast.

Far below the surface rocks fell. Caverns and passageways that had lain open for millions of years were sealed at one critical junction. Tunnels and fissures in the earth's crust were opened and underground rivers were diverted.

Water stopped flowing down and started flowing out...

Chapter 1 – Something Fishy

Hamish and Angus were out in their boat.

The full moon was high and shining brilliant silver light across the whole loch. Moonbeams were glittering upon every ripple on the water.

The other villagers would be soundly asleep by now and all the trout and salmon in the loch were theirs for the taking.

The boat rocked back and forth. Hamish spread his feet out to the edges to steady the motion and placed his hands on the rowlocks. The little craft settled into a gentle lull as the waves and the moonlight sparkled. The night was cold and the air was deathly still.

Beneath the shimmering light the water was inky black. The moonbeams bounced off the surface and the darkness below was left untouched. Hamish stared at the water and felt drawn towards it; as if the deep wanted to swallow him whole. He shook his head.

The road running along the length of the loch was still and empty. No cars had driven passed in the last hour. The only sound was the lapping of the water against the sides of the boat.

Angus had begun baiting the hooks of their fishing rods. Hamish preferred little wiggly worms for the hungry trout but tonight Angus had brought a small jar of salmon eggs with added garlic. The man in the tackle shop had assured him the extra garlic flavour in the water would trigger feeding behaviour in the fish. His steady hands looped the bait onto the hooks.

Hamish watched his older brother for a moment; then stared out across the water again. The dancing moonlight was mesmerising against the jet black of the far shore. The cliffs rose steeply on that side of the loch and shadow of the trees obscured the gloom.

Hamish had heard all the stories about the sea serpent, and had even added a few himself. Pulling the legs of tourists was the local past-time, as well as being good for business so elaborating on rumours of a prehistoric creature in the depths was encouraged, almost expected.

But of course, he wasn't scared. Hamish and Angus had been out on the loch fishing at night many times before and he'd had never seen so much as a fin above the water. The local police and gamekeepers always prosecuted poachers so Hamish took his job as look-out seriously. Being caught stealing fish was far more likely an outcome than meeting a mythical monster.

Angus sat back in the boat and cast off the lines on all the rods. He carefully flicked his wrists back and launched the weight and ball of bait into the water. He did this six times with each of the rods and Hamish heard the quiet 'plop' in the water some distance away.

Now it was time to sit back and wait for a bite.

'Water's high tonight,' grunted Angus.

'Getting higher every time we come out,' replied Hamish, nodding with his head across to the near shore. 'The watermark is climbing up yonder bank. See, passed the seventh step now.'

Angus turned to look at the steps of the dock in the distance. The water was lapping towards the six dry steps up to the top of the small pier.

'Rubbish, man. How can the loch be filling up?' Angus spat back. 'It's hardly rained for weeks and the canal gates are supposed to keep the water level.'

'Aye, but the gates are being flooded as well,' Hamish muttered sullenly. 'Stinks about here too these days,' and he sank back into his corner of the boat.

Time passed slowly.

Usually, there would be an occasional nibble before one of the fish would take the bait. Tonight, there was nothing. The lines were still. The air was silent and even the waves were slow.

Hamish sat bolt upright.

'Did you see that?' Hamish pointed out towards the blackness.

'Away, man. It's your imagination,' Angus was never so easily spooked.

'I'm telling ye, I saw something.' Hamish was almost hanging over the side of the boat, peering out across the water. Angus looked up.

A black mass rose up out of the water before diving underneath the surface silently. The waves created by the creature washed against the little rowing boat.

'There! Did ye see it this time?' Hamish had stood up. His face was as white as the moonlight.

'I'm all wet now,' moaned Angus.

'What? Did that big wave splash on board?' Hamish was still staring at the surface of the loch

'No. I think I've pee'd myself,' replied Angus, trying to pull his wet jeans away from his legs. Steam rose up from his thighs.

'So you did see it!' shouted Hamish, more excited at the prospect of the monster than laughing at his big brother for losing control of his bladder.

'No, no I didn't see anything,' Angus insisted, his hands trembling furiously as he tried to pull in three fishing lines in each hand.

BUMP!

'What was that?' shrieked Hamish, clinging onto the rocking boat. 'Something banged into us. What was it, man?'

'Nothing!' yelled Angus, 'Just start bloomin' rowing, would ye.'

Hamish grabbed at an oar but in his panic he dropped it into the water.

A large dark shape rose from the loch again, sliding elegantly across the surface. It was closer to the boat this time. The body, or just the upper part of the body, for most of the creature remained submerged, swam swiftly towards them. Its dorsal skin looked thick and rugged, with armoured scales overlapping, rammed into the under side of the boat.

Angus dropped to his knees and held onto the rolling boat.

THUMP!

The boat rocked furiously. Hamish lost his balance and toppled over, plunged into the water.

Chapter 2 – High and Dry

'Last one to the top's a hairy baboon!' yelled George, as he pushed harder into his pedals. He was almost at the top whilst Allison was just behind him and Crayon Kenny was lagging at the back.

Beyond the crest of the hill would be the most magnificent view George had ever seen. Little Pump Valley would spread out below and the small town of Little Pumpington would sit to their right. Little Pump Lake would shimmer blue in the centre of the scenery, surrounded to the left by the Little Pump Humps, a series of small hills quaintly named by the locals.

George was ten. He'd lived all his life in Little Pumpington and it still annoyed him that he'd never found another town in the country called Big Pumpington or even a city called Greater Pumpington. He always thought Britain deserved more Big Pumps.

In George's mind, Little Pumpington was the most boring town in the world; nothing exciting ever happened there. Except, of course, the time when George blew up his primary school.

And then there was the mass kidnapping of three thousand old age pensioners!

And also that occasion when his school was swarmed by an epidemic of snot zombies!

But apart from that, nothing exciting had ever happened in Little Pumpington recently. It was already the second week of the summer holidays and there was no sign of any action. George had been hanging out with his friends, Allison and Kenny, feeling bored and fed up with summer already.

The sun had been splitting the sky for weeks, so to alleviate the boredom George suggested that the trio go swimming in Little Pump Lake. It was a beautiful part of the countryside, looked after by the town's conservation group. The lake had been dredged, the rubbish cleared and the water had been transformed the previous summer into a blue lagoon.

Allison had only recently moved to the north east of England so she'd never been to the lake before. George thought she was in for a treat. Kenny's mum had agreed to let him go too, for several reasons. One; she remembered swimming in the lake when she was younger. Two; Kenny needed the exercise, and Three; it might take his mind off sticking strange objects up his nose. That's why the pupils of Little Pumpington Primary christened him 'Crayon Kenny'.

George reached the top of the hill first. He threw down his bike and gazed out at the panoramic expanse beyond. Allison was at his shoulder seconds later. Her brown eyes widened and her mouth dropped.

Eventually Kenny arrived beside them. He was puffing and panting like an old horse and he cursed his mum's attempts to 'fitten him up', as she put it.

George and Allison were still staring at the valley below them.

'What a dump!' gasped Allison.

'Where's the lake?' asked Kenny.

'I thought you said it was beautiful up here?' huffed Allison.

'I thought you said we could go swimming, George?' asked Kenny, starting to feel a little annoyed for cycling up that hill for nothing.

'Where's all the water gone?' George stared in disbelief at the yellow, parched earth that lay where the lake once nestled.

'You mean it's not like this normally?' Allison glanced across at George with narrowing eyes.

'No, of course not,' said George sharply. 'You didn't think I wanted to swim in that muddy little puddle down there.' George pointed to the dark brown patch of sludge sitting in the centre of the dried up lake bed.

''So where's the lake gone then?' Kenny asked again.

'Well, I don't know!' snapped George, becoming irritated that his companions thought it was his fault.

'Maybe somebody's nicked it?' suggested Kenny, trying to soften the mood.

'Don't be stupid! Who could nick an entire lake?' Allison was disappointed and it showed.

'Maybe it was UFO's?' Kenny said. 'Maybe some aliens' home planet was drying up and they came here to borrow some of our water?'

'Borrow water?' Kenny had lit Allison's fuse and George thought it best to move out of the way. 'Borrow water? First of all, Kenny Roberts, even if there were aliens and even if they did need our water, it's not like popping next door to borrow a couple of eggs!'

'They'd not want to give it back,' Allison was on a roll, 'And the government would know about it and this is just another one of your crackpot ideas because you've been watching too many movies again. Honestly, you're worse than George sometimes.'

'Thanks,' shouted George sarcastically from halfway down the hill.

'I didn't mean that in a good way, George.' Allison yelled back.

'Thanks,' smiled Kenny. He quite enjoyed being considered a little eccentric. Then, trying to show his serious side he added, 'Maybe it's dried up in the heat then.'

'I thought of that,' Allison mellowed slightly. 'But it looks like it's been a large lake, judging by the water marks around the sides and I doubt it could dry up in just a few weeks.'

'What's George doing?' said Kenny, changing the subject. He was pointing down towards his friend, who was crawling around on his hands and knees in the centre of the lake bed.

Allison and Kenny started to run down the hill to join him. They bounced and skipped and more than a few times they almost lost control of their legs. They reached the bottom just as George was lying flat on the ground, close to the muddy puddle in the middle.

'Woah, what's that stink?' shouted Kenny, wafting his hand over his face.

'It does pong a bit down here, George,' added Allison, holding her nose.

'Have you farted, mate?' Kenny went on.

George smiled. The air around the lake was whiffy; a stale, sulphuric stench seemed to cling to their clothes.

'It's like rotten eggs,' said Allison, desperate to move back up the hillside.

'It's not actually a farty smell, Kenny,' George said, almost scientifically. 'It's more like wee.'

'Wee? George, really?' Allison was almost ready to believe her nostrils. 'How often do you sniff your own wee and what are you doing crawling about in the dirt, George?'

'The smell's really strong down here,' replied George and as if to prove it he scraped up a handful of dirt in his fingers and pressed it up against his nose. That was all the invitation Crayon Kenny needed. He dropped to his knees and began sniffing the dried earth.

'Uuurgh, it's really honking, George.' Kenny was laughing and screwing up his nose.

'The stink is in the dirt, dude,' George was convinced. 'And you can hear water running underneath the ground.'

Kenny pressed his ear to the ground and nodded. 'It's like a giant flushing toilet under there. Listen.'

Allison was curious now. She dropped to her knees too, still holding her nose tightly. She put one hand out in front of her and tried to lower her ear down to the ground. With one hand squeezing her nostrils, her balance was all wrong and she toppled forward.

George and Kenny saw what was happening. It was in slow motion but there was nothing they could've done about it. Off balance now, Allison tipped to the side. She had a decision to make; let go of her nose and face the stench or try to stop herself falling.

That moment of indecision was enough. Too late, she stretched arms out but she couldn't stop herself squishing face-down in the mud.

'Snrrrrrrrrrt,' sniggered George.

'Prrrrrrp,' stifled Kenny.

'If either of you two even thinks about laughing, I'll…' But that was enough. Allison picked herself up. She was a mess.

The two boys burst out in hysterics; hooting, squealing and pointing at Allison's sludgy face. They could see the look of anger beneath her muddy mask and her face might've been beetroot red, if it wasn't dirty brown.

'I'm warning you!'

But George and Kenny couldn't stop. They were rolling around in the dry dirt now holding their sides, tears streaming down their faces. Allison sat up and brushed a stray strand of hair away from her face to regain some composure. Her shoulders were back, her head held high as she grimly fought to hold her dignity together.

Panting, the lads eventually began to calm down, trying hard not to look at Allison.

'Quite finished, are we?' Allison asked coolly, her face still a brown mud pack.

'Y-yes, yes, s-sorry....' gasped George. 'We just...erm....'

'I suppose it's healthy....for your skin, that is' said Kenny.

'What's healthy about wearing a mud pack that smells like wee?' snapped Allison again, sniffing her fingers.

George thought. 'The dirt really does smell of pee, doesn't it?'

'It is a bit odd,' said Kenny.' 'But did you hear the water flowing underneath, Allison.'

'Well you should have. You had your face in the mud long enough,' he added quietly, under his breath.

Either Allison didn't hear or chose to ignore that quiet remark. 'Yes, I heard it alright,' she stated in a matter of fact fashion. 'There's water flowing somewhere....just not here.' And she spread her arms out around the dried up lake.

'Come on,' said George. 'There's no swimming for us today.'

Chapter 3 – Big Pants

The journey back home took longer than expected. Heading back down the hill wasn't a problem; they made pretty good time until they reached the main road. That was where the difficulties started.

Every time Allison heard a car coming she'd jump off her bike and hide behind a bush or pretend to tie her shoelaces; all the time covering her mud-strewn face.

'You never know who might see me!' she kept shouting at George and Kenny, who'd cycle on in front of her, then wait up further ahead once their conscience kicked in.

When they reached the last bend and Allison's house was in sight, the coast was clear. She stood up on her pedals and sprinted for home.

'She didn't even say 'goodbye',' Kenny muttered. 'I wouldn't be bothered by a little bit of mud on my face.'

'You're not bothered about sticking peas up your nose,' laughed George. 'I think it must be a girl thing.'

'What are we going to do now?' asked Kenny

'Let's go round to see what my Grandpa Jock's up to,' suggested George. 'He's usually got something mental going on.'

'He's barking, your grandpa, isn't he?' said Kenny, following George down a little cul-de-sac.

Grandpa Jock was mental. He had decided years ago that he no longer wanted to be old; why should kids have all the fun stuff, he thought. So he'd given up remembering what age he was (believed to be somewhere between seventy two and ninety eight) and proceeded on with his life as recklessly and irresponsibly as an eight year old.

If anyone ever asked him how old he was, he'd reply 'Older than my teeth but younger than my gums.' Whatever that meant, wondered George. His Grandpa Jock didn't have his own teeth anymore and where were his gums before he was born.

Grandpa Jock had taken up zooming around on George's scooter too. His ginger hair would fly all over the place as he sped around the streets of Little Pumpington; his big purple nose glowing brighter the harder he raced.

He loved technology as much as he loved his bagpipes. Although his bagpipes didn't really love him back. New neighbours in the street where Grandpa Jock lived would think that he was strangling a cat before they got used to the screeching and wailing coming from his house. The police had stopped answering 999 calls when they heard the description of the 'crime' being reported, and where the noise was coming from.

Today, all was quiet when George and Kenny walked up Grandpa Jock's garden path. George opened the back gate and another pungent smell filled their nostrils. This time, it was more pleasant. This time, it was a mixture of honeyed-sweetness, earthy richness and soap.

'What's that pong now?' asked Kenny.

'Porridge!' shouted a voice from inside the kitchen.

'Grandpa?' yelled George.

'George!' the shout back and a bald head popped out from the kitchen door. Not entirely bald though; there was a frame of bushy orange whiskers surrounding a shiny bald patch on the crown. The head was attached to a wiry frame, above a kilt and a spindly pair of legs. The kilt was an immaculate red, green and black tartan.

'And Crayon Kenny too! Hullo lads, in ye come, in ye come,' Grandpa Jock's strong Scottish accent was warm and inviting; a bit like the smell wafting out his back door.

'Grandpa! We don't call him Crayon Kenny anymore,' said George, glancing over apologetically to his friend. 'It's kinda rude.'

'Nonsense, lad,' argued Grandpa Jock. 'Anyone with a talent to stick marbles, brussel sprouts and most of all, crayons up his nose should be proud of the fact. All the boys down the pub think you are a legend, young man.'

Kenny beamed. George could only think his friend was a little peculiar at times. They all stepped through the back door, into the kitchen. There were two large pots simmering on the oven. The kitchen table was strewn with herbs, spices and various bottles and jars of flavourings. A little stool sat under the table.

'What are you cooking, Mr Jock?' asked Kenny, twitching his nose.

'Well, lad,' answered Grandpa Jock, pointing to the first big pan. 'That one is porridge,' he said.

'And that one?' asked Kenny.

'That one's my pants!'

'Uurgh!' both boys shouted together. 'Why are you boiling your pants?'

'Two reasons, really,' Grandpa Jock replied, somewhat sheepishly. 'Don't usually discuss my underpants in public but since you ask.....'

'...First, a good boil wash gets them really clean, you know. What with all the stains and all.' Grandpa Jock was clenching his fists to show the boys how clean he expected his pants to be. 'And second, they need a special wash. They're special pants.'

'Special pants?' The boys were becoming good at talking together, whether they wanted to or not.

'Aye, special pants. Ye see, I've got a problem with....er... my piles.'

'Your piles of what, Grandpa?' asked George, blissfully ignorant.

'No, not piles of anything, lad. Piles....from my bottom.' Grandpa Jock was gesticulating wildly with his hands, trying to mimic something big and clumpy. 'Haemorrhoids!'

'Hemma whats?' asked Kenny, looking puzzled.

'Haemorrhoids, lad. You'll learn about these things as you get older.' Grandpa Jock shuffled his feet uncomfortably. 'Your dad's had them too, you know.'

'But what are they, Grandpa?'

'Well, they're like little lumps and bumps that grow out of your butt, lads.'

George gasped. 'You said 'butt'! Mum will kill you.'

'She doesn't need to know now, does she?' Grandpa Jock winked.

'But what about your lumps and bumps, Mr Jock?' Kenny was intrigued now. As well as his nose, Kenny had been known to hide things in....other places too.

'Well, these little things... kinda grow out your bum, don't they. They can be quite painful at times. And they're really itchy too.' Grandpa Jock stopped his description to have a good scratch, right up the back of his kilt.

'And how do your special pants help?' asked George,

'Aha!' Grandpa Jock held a finger in the air. 'My own special invention, boys. You've heard of 'whoopee cushions', haven't you? Those farting little rubber bags you buy from joke shops?'

'Of course, Grandpa. You bought me one for my birthday once,' replied George.

'Me too,' added Kenny. 'I've got one. You should see my mum's face when I slip it under her chair and lets rip with an enormous fart.' Both boys were chuckling at the hours of fun they'd had.

'Exactly!' And that's where I got the idea for my special pants,' Grandpa Jock was no longer embarrassed about his...er...bottom problem, just excited about his invention. 'Ye see, with piles, it can be a bit painful to sit down sometimes.'

'So I bought two whoopee cushions and sewed them into the back of my pants,' Grandpa Jock's eyes were ablaze. 'That way I've got a big bit of padding under each cheek. I just blow them up before I put them on and seal the end with duct tape.'

'Don't they.....blast off, Grandpa?' asked George. 'That would be a bit embarrassing if you dropped a loud ripper when you sat down on the bus or somewhere.'

'Duct tape, lad. Holds anything in place,' Grandpa Jock nodded wisely.

'Don't they make your bum look big, Mr Jock?' asked Kenny, looking for a flaw in the mad Scotsman's plan.

'Well, I don't blow them all the way up, lad. Just enough for a soft cushion on my tushy.' And at that point Grandpa Jock used a large pair of tongs to pull a sparkling pair of white underpants out of the hot, soapy water. Attached to the pants were two pink rubber bags.

Steam filled the kitchen and Grandpa Jock lobbed the pants into the sink to let them cool off.

Chapter 4 – Porridge

Kenny started laughing. 'Wait till Allison sees your inflatable underwear,' he giggled.

'I'm not showing off my pants to a lady. That would be too rude,' said Grandpa Jock smartly. He may be a windy old eccentric who could play a tune by making pumping noises under his armpits but he had to draw the line somewhere.

'Anyway, Grandpa,' puzzled George. 'I didn't think Scotsmen wore anything under their kilts?'

'When you've haemorrhoids as large as I have, boy, you're glad of the wee bit protection.' Grandpa Jock blew out the side of his mouth in mock relief.

'And what's porridge?' asked Kenny.

'What?' replied Grandpa Jock, snapping out of the pleasurable thought of a cushioned bottom.

'Porridge. You said in the other pot was porridge. So, what's porridge?' asked Kenny again.

'You don't know what porridge is, boy? Where have you been?' exclaimed Grandpa Jock waving his arms around. 'Porridge is the most magical, amazing, wonderful cereal in the world. It's second only to haggis in the taste tests.'

'Yeah, I know what haggis is,' said Kenny, keen to show off his knowledge of Scottish cuisine. 'That's the liver and lungs of a sheep, isn't it? Served up in a stomach lining bag?'

'Spot on, boy' replied Grandpa Jock, pointing his bony finger at Kenny. It was all Kenny could do to stop gagging at the thought of haggis. 'But porridge is simpler. Porridge is just oats and water. Sometimes I add milk.'

'Is that it?' Kenny was hoping for something more creative. George just stood back to allow his grandpa the floor. He'd enjoyed porridge, and haggis many times and he knew how passionate Grandpa Jock was about his favourite foods.

'That's just the start, lad. After that, you can do anything with it. You can add salt and pepper. You English like to add sugar, because you're softies.'

'Hey, watch it, Grandpa,' nodded George. 'I'm English too remember.'

'Part English, lad. Still part Scottish too,' reminded Grandpa Jock. Then he turned back to Kenny, 'Or you can throw in any fruit or olive oil or even haggis.'

'No way,' protested Kenny.

'Yes, way. You can add anything to porridge and it still tastes brilliant. And that's what I'm doing today.'

'What's that, Grandpa?' George was intrigued now. He'd heard, and tasted, most of Grandpa Jocks' porridge recipes but he was up to something new.

'I'm practising my latest recipe,' whispered Grandpa Jock.

'What for?' asked the double act together.

'The World Porridge Making Championships!' he announced, puffing his chest out.

'The what?'

'It's true. Every year, near a city called Inverness in the north of Scotland they hold the World Porridge Making Championships,' Grandpa Jock enthused. 'People from all over the world, America and China and everywhere, gather near Loch Ness to show off their secret recipes. It's a massive event. Last year's winner came from Mexico. They made a chilli and chocolate porridge. It was supposed to be quite tasty.'

'But why are you making porridge today?' asked George, still desperate to know what his grandpa was up to.

'This year......I will be entering the World Championships!'

'Seriously,' gasped Kenny.

'Abso-blooming-lutely, lad! I want to bring the championship crown back to Scotland, where it belongs. And I have just the recipe to win.' Grandpa Jock was now standing on the little stool, holding aloft an imaginary trophy.

'What are you making, Grandpa?'

'Haha, I can't tell you, lad. It's top secret.'

'Oh come on, Grandpa, you can tell us. We can keep a secret.'

Grandpa Jock narrowed his eyes and lowered his voice, 'It's not you I'm worried about, boys. This championship is a cut-throat business. Any one of the competitors would kill for that special edge. You'd be in too much danger if ye knew.'

George and Kenny looked crest-fallen. They'd been hoping to find out what weird creations the mad Scotsman had been conjuring up in his kitchen. Since he had all the contents of his kitchen cupboards scattered across every work surface, along with some of the contents of the bathroom cupboard too, he could be pretty much making anything.

'Coffee and carrots?' asked Kenny, lifting two ingredients from the collection.

'Aftershave?' yelled George, picking up a bottle from the table.

'Tomato sauce and toothpaste?' yelled Kenny.

'Enough, lads, I've said too much.' Grandpa Jock began stuffing all the ingredients back into his cupboards.

The boys were now gutted. Whatever Grandpa Jock was creating had to something a bit magical but they weren't going to find out today. They shuffled their feet sadly. Grandpa Jock sensed their disappointed.

'Tell ye what, though,' said Grandpa Jock, hoping to raise their spirits, 'I will need a couple of helpers up there at the championships, to do the lifting and the carrying.'

George and Kenny stared at each with growing anticipation. 'Ye fancy it?'

'YYYYYYYYYYYES PLEASE!' they shouted in unison and leapt to high-five each other across the kitchen.

Chapter 5 – All Packed

'Come on, George,' yelled George's mum from the living room. 'Get your bag packed, hurry up.'

It was Saturday and George had spent all morning packing and unpacking his rucksack. He'd had a week to get ready and he still couldn't decide what to take. It was summer and the country was in the middle of a heat wave. But Scotland was often wet and there was no guarantee it would stay sunny. And right up north, Scotland often had a climate all of its own.

Then there were the midges to contend with. Midges were tiny little flying insects that lived in warm damp conditions, predominantly in the north. They had the largest teeth to body ratio of any known creature and frequently dined on the exposed flesh of tourists to Scotland.

Scots people were generally immune to the bites of the midges. Or at least they pretended to be. To George, Scottish skin never looked quite the same as anyone else's skin. It was a pale, blue colour, and Grandpa Jock said proudly that this was called peelly-wally.

Peelly-wally was a skin tone particularly associated with people with ginger hair, like George and Grandpa Jock, and burnt easily in strong or even moderate sunshine. Then, for a couple of days, the skin would glow bright red and begin to peel off. Armies of flaking red-heads could be seen wandering the Scottish countryside in the hottest summers, challenging the sun to do its worst. Every fibre of their being was screaming 'Burn me! Bring it on.' George was certain that the entire Scottish nation was a little mad.

But George wasn't entirely Scottish. Should he wear shorts and t-shirts and risk midges and sunburn, or play it safe with jeans and long-sleeved jumpers? Would it rain? Would it stop raining?

Mrs Hansen stomped into George's room. 'Come on, George. What are you messing about at?' she shouted, taking charge of the packing. 'Your grandpa will be here any minute.'

'I'll pack your bag. Go down stairs and sit with your dad.' George's mum had that knack of taking charge of any situation.

Downstairs, George's dad had the knack of being caught picking his nose when he thought no one was watching. George walked into the living room to find his dad knuckle deep.

'Dad!' exclaimed George.

'Better out than in,' answered his father, as he wiped his finger on his newspaper.

'Can I turn the TV over, Dad?' asked George.

'No. I'm watching the news,' replied Mr Hansen.

'No, you're not. You're reading the paper,' answered George, a little miffed.

'Multi-tasking, son. You'll learn how to do that when you pay the bills.' And he looked over his paper to watch the TV screen.

George saw a man with a microphone standing in a field. At least, it looked like a field to begin with but as the camera panned wider George could see it was a dried up lake. The reporter went on....

'All over England, lakes like this one are drying up. It is a drought of biblical proportions and hosepipe bans are in place all over the country. Gardeners tempted to use a hose to water their flowers run the risk of imprisonment....'

'That's like our Little Pump Lake,' said George. 'We went up there a few days ago for a swim but couldn't.

'Shh,' replied George's dad, now intent on staring at the telly.

'....Emergency supplies of bottled water are being

shipped in from all over Europe and fresh tap water is being pumped down from the north of Scotland, which seems largely unaffected by these unprecedented events.'

'Chemical analysis of the soil left behind in the lake beds suggests a high acidic content and scientists are baffled to explain the cause.' The reporter closed off his summary and handed back to the studio.

'Well, at least you'll be able to have a swim up in Scotland,' laughed George's dad. 'You might have to break the ice though,' he chuckled.

'It won't be that cold, will it?' wondered George. 'We're having a heat wave down here.'

'Totally different country, up there. Different climate, different people.'

'But you're Scottish, dad?'

'Only half Scottish, son. Your gran was English,' added George's dad. 'I've lived in Little Pumpington all my life, like you. Your Grandpa Jock moved here when he left the army and married Gran.'

'He was a sergeant major in a pipe band, wasn't he?' said George.

'Yeah, so he says,' then George's dad turned and looked seriously. 'Keep an eye on your grandpa while you're away. You know how he gets a bit....carried away, at times.'

'Sure, Dad,' nodded George.

Just then, George's mum bustled into the living room carrying one neatly packed rucksack.

'There you go,' she said. 'Everything's in there. Jeans, shorts, jumpers, t-shirts, even your swimming shorts and a couple of towels; whatever you'll need.'

George marvelled. Did every mum have the unique ability to fit more stuff into a bag than the space would allow? It shouldn't be technically possible but mums have a way of making bags seem bigger on the inside.

You just need to see inside a lady's handbag.

There was a knock on the back door and Kenny walked straight in. He had a miraculously packed rucksack as well and Mrs Roberts stepped in behind him. Mrs Hansen smiled and went into the kitchen to speak to Kenny's mum. George and Kenny fist-bumped.

'You all set?'

'Yup. You?'

'Yup. Can't wait.'

Occasionally the mumsy voices in the kitchen would be raised and comments were directed through to the boys in the living room.

'Remember to brush your teeth,' and 'Don't let Mr Jock pay for everything, you have your own money,' and 'Put clean pants on every day, George,' and 'Don't stick anything up your nose, Kenny.'

The boys shut off from their instructions.

'When's Allison coming?' asked Kenny.

'Huh! She phoned to say she'd be here in five minutes,' replied George. He wasn't too impressed that Allison had been invited. He was hoping it would've been a lads' holiday. George didn't necessarily fancy Allison; he'd never admit it anyway, she was a friend, a good friend but she was still a girl and George was hoping that the boys could've gone off together. Maybe she was just getting too bossy, grumped George.

Allison had been invited along, mainly by George and Kenny's mums in order to bring a sense of maturity and respectability. George's mum didn't really trust Grandpa Jock to behave himself properly whilst they said George and Kenny were 'too easily led'. Allison was there as the responsible member of the party and George's mum wasn't taking any chances, even going out to buy Allison her very own tent and sleeping bag, just to make sure she could go along.

'That'll be her now,' said George, as the back door opened. Allison walked through to join the boys whilst Allison's mum joined the throng of female voices in the kitchen. Allison carried a neat pink suitcase.

'You alright?'

'Yeah, you?'

'Yeah.'

'Yeah, me too.'

This felt a little awkward. Sure, they were friends, they went to school together and hung out but they'd never been on holiday together. Heck, they'd never even had a sleep-over. Not that Allison's mum would've thought that appropriate.

But Allison had her own tent, as the only young lady of the expedition and she was sensible enough to keep the boys in check. George wondered, does Allison fart at night? They might all be able to hear each other blasting away; no way could the thin walls of two tents keep those eruptions contained. George and Kenny had often enjoyed their trouser trumpets together.

And Grandpa Jock was the master at bottom burps. Silent but violent was his weapon of choice and too often to remember George would find himself and the air around him wrapped in a blanket of rancid cabbages. In fact, sharing a tent with Kenny and Grandpa Jock would be a rather fragrant experience.

'Hey hey, campers!' shouted Grandpa Jock as he barged in the back door. 'Are we ready to rock?!' He was laden with a huge backpack, a tent on top and every tool and implement known to mankind hanging from his kitbag. He even had a six-pole windbreaker strapped to the top of his rucksack.

Grandpa Jock clunked and clanked as he walked. His spade clattered against the tin mugs that were tied to the bottom of his bag. Metal plates hung down too and there were water bottles, cans of food and a little stove swinging around behind him as well.

Kenny noticed that Grandpa Jock's bottom was looking a bit more padded than normal under his kilt and guessed that he'd inflated his whoopee cushion underpants that little bit bigger this morning to last the long train journey.

His hair was flying wildly out to the sides, more than usual, and George took this as a good sign that Grandpa Jock was excited and ready for an adventure.

'Got all your ingredients, Grandpa?' asked George, still totally in the dark as to what the secret recipe was.

'Sure have, young man' replied Grandpa Jock. 'Did you bring all the asparagus I asked for, Allison?'

'Of course, Mr Jock. Packed neatly in my case so the stalks won't break,' said Allison, lifting up her suitcase.

'And the garlic?'

'Yes, Mr Jock.'

'Good girl,' he nodded. 'Knew I could trust you, better than these two Muppets here.' And he signalled over to the boys with a wink.

'Asparagus?' said George.

'Garlic?' said Kenny.

'Muppets?' said George, catching up.

Why hadn't they been involved in the planning and preparation? How come Allison was appointed to the position of principal porridge preparer? The boys, especially George, weren't pleased.

'Now let's get you all along to the station,' urged Allison's mum.

'Remember, it's a change at Edinburgh, then all the way up towards Inverness,' said George's mum.

And Kenny's mum added, 'And Allison, please make sure Kenny doesn't have any peanuts on the train.'

Everyone knew the risks.

Chapter 6 – Loch Ness

The train journey from Little Pumpington to Edinburgh was uneventful, apart from the unfortunate incident with the burst packet of wine gums. The ticket collector hadn't been impressed but Grandpa Jock had almost lost his teeth laughing.

Once aboard the Inverness express the scenery changed massively within the hour. From the flat fields and North Sea coastline into Edinburgh, suddenly hills began to appear, then mountains and vast plunging valleys.

George, Kenny and Allison stared out the window, feeling dwarfed by the steep cliffs and heather covered hillsides. Sharp crags rose up out of the earth and stony shale formed rivers down the mountains. Waterfalls plunged downwards and rivers cascaded over rocks and boulders to reach the bottom of the valley.

It was late afternoon when their train arrived in the little station of Drumnadrochit, a small town on the banks of Loch Ness and a short trek from Inverness. Grandpa Jock was first to jump off the train, feeling a surge of energy now he was back in his homeland.

'Aha, Drumnadrochit! How great is that, George?' beamed Grandpa Jock.

'Drum na what what, Grandpa?' asked George, never having seen letters like this together in the same word.

'It's easy, lad,' laughed Grandpa Jock. 'Say it slowly.'

'Drum,' said George.

'Na,' said Kenny, joining in.

'Draw' prompted Grandpa Jock. 'You pronounce trhe 'dro' like 'draw'.'

'Chit' added Allison. She pronounced it with a hard 'ch'. Grandpa Jock laughed.

'Not chit, like cheese or chops or chunky chips,' Grandpa

Jock explained. 'I suppose it's easier if you pronounce it 'kit'. Drum-na-draw-kit.'

'Drumnadrochit!' shouted George.

'Aye lad, it means Ridge of the Bridge, which sounds pretty cool too, don't ye think?' Grandpa Jock went on.

'So is that Lock Ness over there, Mr Jock?' asked Allison, pointing to the vast body of water stretching away into the distance.

'LOCK Ness! LOCK Ness? It's not Lock Ness, that's far too English. You have to say it like this,' Grandpa Jock's guttural Scottish accent made the word sound easy. 'Loccccchhhhhhhhhhhhhhhhhhhhh'

He hocked a couple of times, as if he was clearing his throat. 'Hockkkkk, hockkkkk,' he said, dragging phlegm and spit up from the back of his mouth. 'Loccchhhhhhhhhhhhhhhhhhhh.'

George was quite used to Grandpa Jock's broad accent but even he felt a little queasy with the amount of frothy growling that was going on.

Allison gave it another go, 'Locuck-uck-uck-yuck.' Her mouth was too dry and the sounds kept sticking.

'You need more moisture in there,' Grandpa Jock suggested. 'As if you're dragging a snotter up from your toes.'

Allison shook her head. 'I'll leave it there, I think,' she said, vowing to try it again later, when no one was listening.

Kenny tried. 'Locccccchhhhhhhhhhhhhhh-hochhhhhhhhhhhhhh-eh huhuhuhuh.'

'Quick, he's choking,' shouted Grandpa, and George was first to react. He quickly slapped his friend between the shoulder blades.

'Ugh huh ah huh,' Kenny coughed up a huge ball of snot and spat it into a field with a fearsome gob.

'Does everyone up here speak with an accent, Mr Jock?' asked Allison trying to change the subject.

'Well, almost everyone, lassie.'

'It must be risky asking for directions,' giggled George.

'Yeah, we'd be washing phlegm out your hair for a week afterwards,' laughed Kenny.

Allison was beginning to wonder why she'd come along on this lads' holiday after all and she walked briskly off the platform and along the road towards the campsite.

Grandpa Jock winked to George and Kenny, 'Best tone it down a little, boys.' And he hurried to catch up with Allison. George and Kenny stared at each other and started to snigger.

'Maybe you need to be over seventy to understand women properly,' chortled George.

*

By the time they'd reached the campsite the plan was agreed. Grandpa Jock had told Allison that it didn't really get dark in the north of Scotland until close to midnight so there was plenty of time to put the tents up.

He'd handed Allison some money and persuaded her to take the boys off to buy ice cream. It would be best to allow them to let off some steam since they'd been cooped up in that train for a few hours. And once the tents were up, they could all go into the village for fish and chips.

A suitable spot was found, the bags were dropped off and Grandpa Jock started to unpack the tent poles.

'Are you sure you can manage on your own, Grandpa?' asked George, more out of politeness than helpfulness. He had his mind set on the ice cream.

'I'll be fine, lad,' growled Grandpa Jock, 'I've put up more of these things than you've had hot dinners.'

George, Allison and Kenny wandered off towards the village. For a Saturday, the place seemed quite quiet.

Chapter 7 – Tall Tales and Tents

The evening was warm with a fresh breeze blowing in off the water. George, Allison and Kenny stared out across the loch, finishing their ice cream cones. The water was still and there were a few boats bobbing about, way off in the distance.

'Do you think there really is a Loch Ness Monster?' asked Kenny.

'It's probably all a big joke to keep the tourists coming,' replied Allison cynically.

'My Grandpa Jock is not sure either way,' answered George. 'There's been thousands out sightings but no real proof. I suppose we'll never know until some evidence turns up, you know, officially.'

'My dad says there's this photograph, taken way back in the thirties,' said Kenny, 'That's meant to look like the head of a monster. And it was taken by a surgeon too, so everyone believed him.'

'Have you seen it, Kenny, the photograph I mean,' asked Allison curiously.

'Yeah, my dad showed me it on the Internet.'

'AND?'

'I thought it looked like a close up of an elephant's trunk, actually,' replied Kenny, somewhat disappointingly. 'But if it was taken from a distance, I suppose it might've looked like a sea serpent's head. You just can't tell.'

'I can tell ye, alright,' said a voice from behind them. 'I saw it. Last week. Pulled me into the water, it did.'

George, Allison and Kenny turned in amazement. Standing there in khaki shorts and a dirty Scotland football jersey was a small boy with bright red hair. Now George's hair was ginger but this lad's thatch was positively flaming.

'Who are you?' asked George.

'I'm Hamish,' said the boy. He was smaller in height that George but he looked slightly older, about twelve or thirteen.

'And you think you've seen a monster, Hamish, have you?' queried Allison. She wasn't about to start listening to the wild stories of the locals. 'And for ten pounds, no doubt you'll show us where you saw it?'

'Naw, I'm serious. I don't want your money,' shrugged Hamish. 'But I just think you should be careful, that's all. There've been a lot of sightings of the monster recently'

'What happened to you then?' asked George.

'I was fishing with my big brother, Angus,' said Hamish. 'And this big beast came swimming up to us and banged into our boat.'

'And it reached up and pulled you in, I suppose?' asked Allison, raising an eyebrow.

'Well, sort of,' replied Hamish, looking a little unsure now. 'But it did bump our boat.'

'Did it?' asked Allison.

'Well, something hit the boat.'

'And you went into the water?' suggested George. 'Did you see it?'

'I definitely saw something,' insisted Hamish. 'It was dark though.'

'And what about your brother?' said Kenny. 'Did he see anything?'

'Naw, he says he didn't. But he wet his trousers so I'm sure he saw something that frightened him.'

'But he's denying it now?' said George.

'Aye, he says he doesn't want to talk about it,' shrugged Hamish. 'And nobody will believe me. Stories of sightings are ten-a-penny about here.'

'So how did you get out of the water then?' asked George, trying to piece it all together.

'Angus pulled me out and then we rowed back to shore. I'd lost an oar though so it took a while,' admitted Hamish.

'Right, hold on,' declared Allison. She had pieced it together! George and Kenny took a tiny step backwards. They knew Allison was about to go for it.

'You think you saw something but it was dark. There was a bump on the boat but you're not sure what it was. You just fell in the water and your brother lost control of his bodily functions. What age is he? Two?'

'Naw, Angus is eighteen. And at least he only wet himself. It might've been a jobby.'

'A jobby?' quizzed Kenny. 'What's a jobby?'

George tutted. 'Have you never heard of a jobby before? It's one of Grandpa Jock's favourite words.'

'It's a good Scottish word for a poo,' added Hamish proudly.

Allison sighed. 'Is that the best story you can come up with? I think it needs a more padding for the tourists.'

'I might've guessed you wouldn't believe me either,' said Hamish as he turned away.

'Hang on,' said Kenny, pointing at Allison. 'She doesn't believe you but we're still interested.' Kenny now pointed between himself and George.

'Still gullible, you mean,' replied Allison.

'It's just another example of uncorroborated evidence,' said George. 'We want to believe you but there's just no solid proof.'

'Why don't ye come with me tonight? Let's look for proof,' said Hamish in a hushed tone.

'What? Go with you? That sounds like a right scam,' snapped Allison. 'Going out on a boat with you and your brother? You'll probably abandon us on an island out there on the lake and steal all our money.'

'Right, will ye tell her, boys?' Hamish was losing his

patience with Allison now.

'It's a loch,' said George quietly, 'not a lake.'

'And my brother's too scared to go out in the boat again. I need to take somebody with me,' argued Hamish. 'And anyway, there's only one island on Loch Ness and that's right down the south.'

'Hey, maybe Grandpa Jock could come with us?' suggested Kenny.

'That's not a bad idea, Crayon!' George was getting excited now, forgetting his promise not to call Kenny 'Crayon'.

'Wait, wait, wait,' said the girly voice of reason. 'We can't go tonight. Your Grandpa Jock has his competition tomorrow. He'll want a good night's sleep.' George knew Allison was right. It was the Porridge World Championships the following day and Grandpa Jock was taking it very seriously.

'What about the following night?' asked Kenny.

'It would be a pretty cool adventure,' added George.

'But what about Mr Jock? You haven't even asked him,' said Allison, trying to think up excuses but realising she was on the losing side.

George chuckled. 'I don't think it would be too difficult to persuade Grandpa Jock to go Nessie hunting.'

*

They agreed to meet Hamish the following morning at the competition. Hamish said an entire Highland gathering had developed around the Porridge World Championships and for the first time the competition was being held on a Sunday. There was a carnival atmosphere about the festival, with tents and stalls, games and amusements and a fairground, all built up around the world famous porridge contest.

George, Allison and Kenny were in high spirits when they made their way back to the campsite. The field was now a sea of tents and caravans and Grandpa Jock was nowhere to be seen.

'Where did we leave him again?' asked George, standing with his hands on his hips, looking around.

'I can't remember,' replied Kenny.

'I think it's this way,' said Allison and she marched off between the first two tents on the outer edge of the campsite.'

#%@#*&@@$!

A loud, yet muffled grunting emanated from the centre of the ring of tents.

'He's over here,' nodded Allison, still walking forward.

&*##@!!!%&**?!#! The agitated muttering continued.

'Yes, I think that would be him now,' agreed George, looking at Kenny and shaking his head.

Allison turned passed the last tent and stopped abruptly. George and Kenny walked right into the back of her.

In the middle of the field, a large, empty ring of grass had developed. Campers were edging their tents away from the centre, trying to inch back into the safety of numbers.

'Grandpa?' asked George, unsure of what he was seeing.

At the heart of the grassy isolation was a jumping tent. Or a man inside a tent. Or a tent-man.

The tent certainly wasn't put up, not in the conventional

sense. There were arms and legs and tent poles kicking and punching and flying in every direction and the worst possible language was being furiously grumbled from inside the canvas.

Other campers, who were unfortunate enough to stumble into this ring of mayhem, quickly gave the area a wide berth. They'd never seen a man trying to fight his way out of a big blue bag before and now didn't seem like a good time to start.

'Grandpa?' George said a little louder as Kenny pushed him towards the mass of limbs, poles and outer coverings.

'Bloomin'.... blinking..... blasted....' followed by a series of inaudible mutterings, 'stinkin'.... stupid.... smelly tent!'

'Er, can I help you, Grandpa?' George was still a little scared to go too close.

'Ah George, about time, laddie,' said Grandpa Jock, his ginger head popping up from inside the tangle of canvas. 'I nearly had it up there a wee while ago.'

Grandpa Jock's face was purple and his nose looked ready to explode. His hair was sticking out in all directions and his moustache was bushy and pulsing up and down. The old Scotsman was puffing hard.

George began to slowly untangle Grandpa Jock. Allison and Kenny saw that it was safe to move in and they started to lend a hand too. Soon, Grandpa Jock was removed from the twisted mass of tent poles, ropes and canvas and he looked positively relieved. Well, almost.

'I'll just need to....er....go to the loo, just now, I think' he said, 'I've been stuck in there for a couple of hours, and I'm kinda....er... bursting.' Grandpa Jock shuffled a few steps away from the man-eating tent, then turned and sprinted towards the campsite's toilet block.

*

It didn't take Allison, George and Kenny long to finish off putting the tent up. Well, mainly Allison, who seemed to have a vision of what the finished structure should look like. George just followed her directions whilst Kenny occasionally rolled about on the grass, clutching his hands. He was no good at hammering in the tent pegs.

By the time Grandpa Jock had returned from the toilet, he was calm and collected and the tent was up. It looked pretty sturdy too.

'Well done, Allison,' acknowledged Grandpa Jock, 'I knew I could trust you.'

George and Kenny just stared at each other open mouthed. The tent was impressive; a long, slim two bedroom tent with a central cabin section, separating out the sleeping areas and a low porch at the entrance.

'Now, if you excuse me,' said Grandpa Jock determinedly, 'I have some work to do.'

He picked up his bag of ingredients, the small primer stove and a couple of pans that were attached to his rucksack and he snuck round the back of the tent. A moment later he trotted round to the front again, lifted the windbreaker and the mallet, which was dropped at Kenny's feet, and ran back behind the tent again.

After several minutes of banging, thumping and cursing, George, Kenny and Allison decided to risk peeping around the edge of the tent. Around the back, they saw that Grandpa Jock had now hammered himself into the centre of the windbreaker and he was surrounded by brightly coloured canvas. He saw them staring and ducked down into his little den.

'What are you playing at, Grandpa?' shouted George.

'I can't be too careful, lad,' replied Grandpa Jock from inside his hidden kitchen. 'This recipe is top secret and I don't want people spying on me.'

'Now, here's some cash,' and a wrinkly old hand popped up from the centre of the windbreaker holding a twenty pound note. 'Go and get yourself some chips.'

George took the money, the hand disappeared and the three children set off for the chip shop.

*

As they returned to the campsite with two fish and chips, a sausage supper and a spicy haggis, and Kenny threatening to 'have fun' with his pickled onion, they saw thick smoke curling up from behind the tent. The air was sweet and poignant, and occasionally filled with a small explosion and burst of flame. Now and again a blue cloud would rise up from within Grandpa Jock's secret camping laboratory and a swear word would be uttered.

George looked at Allison and just shook his head. 'Don't ask.'

Chapter 8 – The World Porridge Making
Championships

'How did you sleep last night, Mr Jock?' asked Allison, who was first up, most organised and already cooking breakfast on the little primer stove.

'Terrible,' Grandpa Jock muttered. 'I'm a bit nervous about this competition today and those two kept me awake half the night farting away. The tent was like a smelly sauna.'

'I know. I heard,' tutted Allison, glad the stench hadn't penetrated through to her compartment.

'What are you making for breakfast, lass?' asked Grandpa Jock, impressed that Allison had the confidence and gumption to get the food on.

'Porridge, of course,' she replied. 'It's the one thing we have plenty of, Mr Jock. But I was going to fry off some crispy bacon and mix them in together.'

'Haha, now you're talking, lassie,' laughed the old Scotsman, 'We'll make a highland chef out of you yet.'

'How do you think you'll get on today,' asked Allison as she stirred the big pot of oatmeal and simmering milk.

'Oh, I dunno,' Grandpa Jock shook his head and for the first time, Allison thought he looked genuinely worried. 'We're up against some stiff competition. Last year's winners have been experimenting with porridge nachos with salsa, which sounds a wee bit tasty.'

'And there's a new German team entered for the first time this year. Their speciality is Black Porridge Gateaux, which might be quite exciting.'

'Well, whoever wins, Mr Jock, at least you'll do your best and we'll have some fun trying.'

Allison had moved the hot pan off the stove and set the strips of bacon out on the griddle pan. Now, the aroma of

wafting bacon was drifting into the darkest recesses
of the smelly tent and George and Kenny were beginning
to surface.

'What time is it?' was the grunt from the boys'
compartment.

'Time you lazy mongrels were up out of your pits,'
laughed Grandpa Jock and he winked across at Allison.

'What day is it?' groaned Kenny.

'Sunday, you eejits! Now get your scrawny wee butts over
here. Allison's made us some breakfast.'

'Allison's made us some breakfast, has she?' mumbled
George, under his breath. 'Allison's just great, isn't she?
Allison's little Miss Wonderful, nah, nah, na-na-nah!'

But the delicious breakfast smell was enough to drag the
boys from their sleeping bags and soon the bacon porridge
was scoffed by all four of them. George eyed Allison
suspiciously, what was she up to? he thought, getting up
early to make everybody's breakfast? Kenny was oblivious
to George's suspicions and used his last rasher of bacon to
wipe the inside of the porridge pot.

One by one they trotted off to the shower block to get
ready for the day and by the time Grandpa Jock had
washed the dishes in Loch Ness, cleaned the little stove
and prepared his ingredients hamper, they were all set.

As they walked to the fairground, Grandpa Jock was
getting excited again and talking non-stop. George was
worried his grandpa would wet himself, as he'd been known
to do, before he could even start to make his porridge.

'The competition's been going nearly thirty years,' he said,
'but a few years back there was a split in the organising
committee.' He went on, not pausing for breath.

'The original event was only about making proper
porridge, with just oats, water and salt, real easy, like - in a
town called Carrbridge, not far from here.' Grandpa Jock

was talking faster and his accent was taking on a northern twang. 'It was just about the best tasting porridge in the olden days.'

'That award was called The Golden Spurtle, named after the long, fat wooden spoon used for stirring porridge hundreds of years ago. See, if ye don't stir your porridge it goes all lumpy.'

George whispered to Kenny, 'I think it must be his nerves.'

'There was a speciality section back then too, which was always looked down upon,' Grandpa Jock was almost skipping as he spoke, 'But then celebrity chefs starting getting involved and speciality porridge took over. There was a breakaway competition and they moved here to Drumnadrochit.'

'Now, there are teams of chefs from all over the world taking part.'

They stopped at the main gate to the playing fields, at a sign that read 'Competitors Only', which pointed round behind the big marquee. There were lots of smaller tents, stands and gazebos being set up as stall holders began to display their wares, hoping to sell a few souvenirs to the growing crowd.

A large, gruff Scotsman in a kilt with a bushy beard stood watching the spectators arrive. He was leaning on an old hunting stick with a 'Y' shaped notch on the top. He was one of the organisers. At least, the boys guessed he was one of the organisers because he wore a large yellow rosette that read 'Organiser'. Grandpa Jock walked up to him.

'Morning. We're competing in the porridge championships. Can we just go straight into the main tent?' he asked.

'Morning. Aye, just follow the path round to the back. Watch out for the big oat truck, mind.'

'The oat truck?' asked George.

'Aye, oat truck, lad,' said the big man. 'With oats in it. We're the World Porridge Championships; we need plenty of the natural ingredients.'

'Oh, good stuff,' said Grandpa Jock, getting excited again. 'My name's Grandpa Jock, by the way,' and he thrust his hand out as an introduction.

'Delighted to meet you, Jock,' replied the big bearded man, reaching out and shaking his hand. 'My name's Laird Baird.'

'The Laird? Wow!' gasped Allison. 'So you own all this land then.' George didn't want to admit that he didn't know what a laird was.

'Aye, lassie, most of it, anyway.' Laird Baird turned to Grandpa Jock again. 'Is this your first competition then, Jock?

'Oh aye,' replied Grandpa Jock, 'And I'm fair looking forward to it.'

'Good, I hope you enjoy it,' nodded Laird Baird. 'It's the first time we've held the competition on a Sunday. Caused a bit of a stooshie up here, like.'

'What's a stooshie?' whispered Kenny.

'I think it means 'a fight or an argument,' replied George, a little unsure.

'Most people have been reasonable about it,' Laird Baird continued. 'But there's a few head-bangers who think the Sabbath should stay sacred even though we've got some special visitors arriving tomorrow. The Guinness Book of Records people are coming on Monday for our attempt to make the world's biggest bowl of porridge'

'That sounds impressive,' said Grandpa Jock nodding 'How big is going to be?'

'Well, the current record is nearly 1000 litres of porridge, set by a team from Edinburgh,' Laird Baird explained, getting excited at the prospect. 'But we're planning to fill the entire harbour with 22 tonnes of oats.'

'Twenty two tonnes!' yelled George and Kenny.

'Do you think that'll be enough?' laughed Grandpa Jock, shaking his head in amazement.

By now, Laird Baird was shaking his walking stick in the air and spreading his arms out wide, yelling....

'AYE, 22 TONNES OF PORRIDGE, MAN. THAT'S ENOUGH TO FEED THE ENTIRE VILLAGE FOR A YEAR'

'Well, I wish you all the best,' said Grandpa Jock and Laird Baird slapped him heartily on the shoulder as Grandpa Jock, George, Allison and Kenny set off down the path. 'And tomorrow you can join us, if you like, for our world record.'

'I think we will,' agreed Grandpa Jock, then he cocked his head. 'Can't argue, the man likes his porridge.'

'The man's a wee bit mad, Grandpa,' added George.

*

As they walked behind the main marquee, they were met with a massive, articulated dump truck, which sat proudly on a four axle, eight wheel base. Each wheel was taller than George's head. The chassis had a large green dumper body mounted to the truck's frame and whole rear end was raised and lowered using a hydraulic ram, fitted under the front of the truck bed.

Grandpa Jock whistled low under his breath. 'Look at that big beauty.'

'It's just a big truck, Grandpa. No big deal.' George shrugged.

'I used to drive trucks like this when I was in the army.' Grandpa Jock's eyes were glazing over as he thought back.

'What? Did you deliver porridge to the troops too,' laughed George, as he nudged Kenny.

'Well, I think it's cool that you can drive big trucks like this one, Mr Jock,' said Allison, refusing to let George's lack of enthusiasm spoil the moment.

'Well, na-na-na-na-na, na-na-na' muttered George childishly. 'She's really getting on my nerves, Kenny,' he whispered.

'Let it go, George. It's not a problem,' replied Kenny, walking into the tent.

Grandpa Jock and Allison were giggling together in front, as George and Kenny dragged behind. Inside the big tent was warm and musty. Twenty tables were set up with two ring gas hobs sitting on top of each one. Tubes fed down beneath the tables to large gas cylinders below.

George pointed to the first stall. The sign above read 'Espagne – Spain' and a group of three agitated little cooks ran around behind their table, all shouting orders at each other. There was another sign on the front of their table that read 'King Prawn Porridge Paella'.

Kenny pretended to stick two fingers down his throat and made a yakking noise.

The next table was the Germans, a quartet of big fat chefs with long handlebar moustaches, lederhosen and funny hats with feathers stuck in them. They were using big bars of cooking chocolate, jars of chocolate powder, cherries and lots of cream.

George and Kenny kept walking, although George had to pull Kenny away from the cherries. Really, thought George, anything small, round and marble sized!

They walked passed signs that read Porridge Pancakes and Pumpkin Porridge. There were chefs and assistants running around behind the tables, frantically working to create their own specialities.

There was even one sign that read 'Penguin Porridge Pancakes.'

George nudged Kenny again. 'I hope they mean the

biscuits and not the little flightless birds.'

Two television cameramen ran passed, forcing George and Kenny to jump back, as they filmed two little old ladies closely inspecting each of the dishes, alongside an elderly vicar, who looked as if he needed a good wash, as they wandered by the tables.

Finally, at the last stall before Grandpa Jock's stood a group of three men wearing long white lab coats. They didn't look like chefs, more like scientists and they all had goggles on. They stood together with their clip-boards, pointing at a smoking vat of blue sugar. At least, George hoped it was sugar.

One of the scientists then snapped the lock down on a vacuum-sealed glass jar and turned a valve on a gas cylinder marked 'carbon dioxide'. George heard a hissing sound and the mixture inside began to bubble. The sugar granules hopped and popped as the pressure inside began to rise and congealed crystals formed around the lining of the giant jar.

Kenny and George stepped back, worried that the bubbling vat would explode.

''Scuse me, lads,' said Laird Baird, from behind them. The big organiser in the kilt stepped around the boys. And they noticed the Scotsman was grumbling.

'What about this lot, eh? Their team name wasn't good enough, wanted it changed to something fancier, didn't they, lads? With a slogan and all.'

George and Kenny looked up at the new team name.

'Science USA,' it read, 'The Geeks Shall Inherit the Earth.'

'Bloomin' Yanks,' Laird Baird continued, as he pinned the name of their speciality porridge onto the front of their table.

'Popping Space Porridge' it read.

George looked along the front of the entrants' tables

and wondered if Grandpa Jock had known how stiff the competition was going to be?

At the final table, Grandpa Jock and Allison had unpacked the large bag of ingredients they'd brought and Allison was already stirring a little copper pan that sat on one of the hob rings.

'That's it, lass, 'said Grandpa Jock, looking over her shoulder. 'Just reduce it to a gentle simmer.'

'What's that?' asked George, a little miffed again that Grandpa Jock had asked Allison to assist him with the cooking. Of course, George had almost burnt his mum and dad's house down, in what was now known as 'the toaster incident' but it was the thought that counted.

''Brown sugar,' replied Allison, unaware of George's envy.

Grandpa Jock leaned across the front of the hob and threw some violet flowers into the mixture and winked across at George. 'Purple heather, lad. Lovely flavour and it was Allison's idea.'

'Remember, we'll have to add the raisins right at the end, lass,' said Grandpa Jock turning to Allison.

Next, he took out two large bunches of asparagus stalks, held together with a tartan ribbon. He stood the little bushels on the front of the table and admired his handiwork. He beckoned George in closer, taking him into his confidence and whispered. 'Camouflage, lad. Eating too much asparagus will turn your wee-wee green and it'll put those spies off my scent.' He nodded across to the table of science-geeks.

'Spies, Grandpa? They're more like wimpy chemistry teachers,' snapped George, almost refusing to be part of his conspiracy.

'We'll see, son. We'll see.' And Grandpa Jock returned to his big bag of oatmeal.

Just as George and Kenny were getting ready to leave

the tent, the big organiser returned with another couple of
sheets of paper in his hand.

'There you go, Jock, don't say I'm no good to ye.' And he
slotted in the name plate above the table and pinned the
recipe title to the front.

'The Jock Squad' read the name plate.

'Sounds reasonable,' shrugged Kenny. George rolled
his eyes and looked down at the name of Grandpa Jock's
recipe. He didn't feel part of The Jock Squad and he was
stewing over Allison's promotion.

'Heather-Honeyed Haggis Porridge with a Whisky-
Caramel and Raisin Sauce' read the title, somewhat
impressively. Kenny nodded. George turned and headed
out of the tent.

'What's the matter, mate?' Kenny shouted after his friend.

'Ah, nothing,' George grumped. 'I just feel like a second
class citizen with that old duffer and little miss smarty-pants
in there.'

'Don't take it so serious, George,' said Kenny, with a little
more wisdom that George really gave him credit for.

George and Kenny never really spoke seriously; it was
more about nonsense with them. 'I mean, I think your
Grandpa likes Allison because she reminds him of your
big sister. Henrietta's all grown up now so Allison's her
substitute, not yours.'

George was surprised by Kenny's maturity. 'Are you
sure?' he asked.

'No. I'm just talking out of my butt, as usual,' joked Kenny.
'Course I'm sure, you bozo! Now, let's go have some fun at
this fair.'

Chapter 9 – Pretty Poetry

Ten minutes later, the boys were sadly disappointed.

They'd walked all the way around the tents and stalls and there was little in the way of 'cool' entertainment. The rides didn't start until later that afternoon and the stalls were selling homemade jams, knitted doilies, pots, pans and porridge equipment.

'I mean, look at all this pap!' raged George. 'It's all a load of tosh and souvenir rubbish for the tourists.'

'But we are tourists,' said Kenny, tripping over a tent rope.

'I know but not real tourists. The blooming amusements don't start for another three hours and the only bit of sport at any these stalls, apart from the porridge competition, is a poetry contest.'

'Poetry?!' gaped Kenny.

'I know! That's how bad it is,' yelled George. 'We're men of the world, Kenny. Adventurers. Monster hunters, well, we will be tonight. We're certainly not interested in poncy poetry.'

'Hey lads, how you doing?' George and Kenny turned. Walking up behind them was Hamish, his hair flaming in the morning sunshine.

'We're bored, Hamish,' shouted Kenny. 'There's nothing to do here.'

'Here. Scoff this for a start.' And Hamish handed them a bar of toffee each. 'I love this stuff, man. I eat it all time.'

'What is it?' asked George, chewing into the soft, sticky confection.

'Highland toffee,' replied Hamish. 'It's brilliant! I eat it for my breakfast and everything.'

'Itsh very shweet,' said Kenny, finding it difficult to speak with his gums wedged together.

'I bet thish ish why Grandpa Jock'sh teeth fell out,' struggled George.

'Ach, ya southern softies,' said Hamish. 'I never go anywhere without some. Now, what about a wee bit o' mischief.'

George stopped and stared. That's something his Grandpa Jock would say. Could this little half-pint Highlander be onto something?

'What are you planning, Hamish?' asked George, with a knowing glint in his eye. George could sniff out a mad plan half a mile away.

'I'm about to enter the poetry competition!' announced the wee man.

'What!?' yelled George and Kenny together. 'Poetry's for girls!' said George. 'We thought you meant some mad stuff, man.'

'Just have patience, lads. Let me explain.'

George and Kenny each raised an eyebrow. They weren't holding out much hope and so far Hamish hadn't even so much as talked a good game, never mind come up with the goods.

'Old Miss McParvis judges the poetry, OK?' George and Kenny nodded but had no idea who Old Miss McParvis was.

'She's one of the teachers down at the school,' said Hamish, as if reading their minds. 'She's very polite, prim and proper but smells like lavender. Always likes things to be precise. Even saying 'dash it' in front of her would be considered a crime.'

'Okaaaayyyyyyyyy,' said George and Kenny together nodding, in a slow, drawn out agreement.

'Well, last year Angus entered a poem in the competition and Miss McParvis wet her breeks,' laughed Hamish.

'Her breeks,' said George.

'Aye, her breeks,' Hamish was hopping up and down, laughing to himself. 'You know, her knickers, her pants, man. She wet her pants.'

'There's much more incontinence in the Highlands than I would've thought,' mused George.

'But that's the point, George' Hamish held his hands up appealing to George's wicked sense of humour. 'She wasn't expecting anything that rude in her nice poetry contest so we took her by surprise.'

'That's not a bad idea, Hamish,' said George, nodding. 'I like it, I like it. Now, where's Angus?'

'Eh, just a wee problem there,' Hamish hesitated. 'He doesn't want to come out the house now.'

'What?! How old did you say he was?' gasped Kenny.

'Er, eighteen,' replied Hamish. 'But I think he got a real scare the other night. He's not well.'

'So what are we going to do about a freaky poem?' asked Kenny. 'I want to see this old dear wet herself for a laugh.'

Hamish sniggered. 'You're sick, Kenny.'

'Who needs Angus?' said George defiantly. 'We can write our own poems!'

'Who can?' replied Kenny. 'Not me, that's for sure. I've never written poetry in my life.'

'It's easy,' said George. 'It's just about finding something to say and rhymes to say it with.'

'I knocked out a couple earlier,' Hamish was talking quietly now.

'What? Why didn't you say before, you sweaty sock? Let's here them.'

'Naw, they're rubbish, really,' replied Hamish.

'C'mon Hamish, you're amongst friends,' Kenny tried to reassure him but was secretly hoping he wouldn't have to write his own poem.

'Alright, here goes with the first one,' and Hamish cleared his throat and flicked out a piece of paper that was in his back pocket.

'Roses are red. Violets are blue,' he sang lovingly.

'Your breath stinks of fish and your bum smells like poo.'

Kenny and George giggled. It was slightly funny but it was not the poem to cause an ancient old teacher to soil her undergarments.

'Not bad, Hamish,' applauded George. 'But I still think we need something better.'

Hamish held up the sheet of paper in front of Kenny and asked 'Well, do you think this one will do?' pointing to his second poem.

Kenny's eyes nearly popped out of his head, as he read. His jaw dropped. 'It certainly rhymes well.'

'What's that you're doing? Poetry contest, is it?' said a voice from over their shoulders.

Allison had snuck up behind them and had been listening for a couple of seconds. Grandpa Jock was leaving his honey haggis to set for a couple of hours so Allison was temporarily relieved of her culinary duties.

'I saw that poetry contest stall earlier, when I came up before breakfast,' said Allison.

'Oh you would,' snapped George.

'I just wanted to say that I've finished my entry,' Allison looked dismayed. 'I wondered if you wanted to hear it, that's all.'

Kenny looked at George, who had his arms folded and was staring off in the other direction. Kenny added, 'Sure, Allison. Let's here your poem then.'

Allison's mood lightened and she too, brought out a sheet of paper from her back pocket. George still kept his arms folded but had turned towards the group again.

'The purple-headed heather,' Allison began.

'That grows upon the moor.'

'Will point the way to your true love,' she continued.

'Of that there's nothing surer.'

George yakked. Kenny turned his back, stifling his laughter. Allison went on...

'You cannot say. You cannot tell.'

'Your love could not be truer.'

'But your true love cannot accept your gift,'

'Because he's just too immature.' And Allison bowed to Hamish's wild applause. George and Kenny were shaking their heads in disbelief.

'That'll never win,' said George.

'That teacher is more likely to throw up in a bucket, than wet her pants in disgust,' added Kenny.

'I liked it,' gushed Hamish, staring longingly at Allison. George was sure Allison might've tried to bat her eyelashes at that moment so he stepped in quickly.

'Right, we have no choice, Crayon, old chap,' announced George standing in the centre of the group. 'We'll have to write some poetry now,' he declared. 'We'll have to write the most filthy, yucksome, vomit-worthy, disgusting bag of rhymes that ever set foot on a page. Not only has our poetry to upset the urine out of an old lady, but it also must overcome the sickly-sweet, sugary pap that every girl in this village is going to come up with.'

'Kenneth, let us retire to our tent with our thinking caps on,' and George swept his arm majestically across the field and he strode back towards the campsite. Kenny followed quickly behind. Hamish stayed to stare at Allison and simpered a little. Allison shuffled awkwardly.

'It's time I was back in the porridge tent,' she said, making her excuses and skipping back to the big marquee. Hamish sighed.

Chapter 10 – Not So Pretty Poems

For the next two hours George sat in his tent, scribbling furiously. He was not going to let Allison's sloppy slush win that contest, or at least, not without a yucky fight. Kenny had scratched his poem out in about five minutes and had gotten bored waiting on George to finish his masterpiece. Kenny had gone up to the porridge marquee to offer Allison and Grandpa Jock a helping hand.

'She can't win,' muttered George to himself. 'Mushy stuff like that has no place in good poetry,' he said.

'And anyway, did you see how she smiled at him,' he grimaced. 'Oh, look at the new boy,' George was squeaking like a girl, pretending to be Allison, 'look at me showing off in front of the new boy.'

'Just because he's a teenager and has the brightest head of hair ever, and he's seen the Loch Ness Monster,' growled George, working himself into a frenzy.

'He's still a midget and his brother wets himself!'

George slammed shut the little pocket book he'd been writing in. His poem was a masterpiece and he was sure the locals would appreciate the use of some Scottish words. Grandpa Jock would certainly approve.

'This will knock their socks off,' he concluded as he left the tent.

*

By the time George walked back up to the playing fields again the World Porridge Making Championships and the fete were in full swing. Throngs of locals, tourists and visitors were milling around the stalls and even the fairground rides had started up. But George wasn't interested in anything else.

The poetry competition had gathered quite a crowd. George saw Kenny, Allison and Hamish waiting by the steps to the stage. He was just in time.

An elderly man in a dirty white dog collar beneath his tweed jacket stepped onto the stage. He had leather patches on the sleeves of his jacket. He gave the microphone a couple of taps and a shrill whistled echoed from the speakers.

'That's the Reverend McVicars,' declared Hamish, somewhat obviously. 'He works at the church.'

'Looks like he needs a bit of a wash,' remarked Allison.

Kenny laughed. 'George, you should've written a poem called Reverend McVicars and his Dirty, Holy Knickers. That would've been good.'

'And his collar could do with some bleach,' added Allison.

'And his pants, I'll bet,' sniggered George.

'Er hullo, everyone.....Is this thing on? Aye, Ok, hullo everyone and welcome to the Drumnadrochit Poetry Contest. After last year's...er...wee accident....,' announced the reverend.

'Literally,' whispered Hamish.

'...this year's event will take a different format. Miss McParvis is still too nervous to read any poems... so I will be leading the panel of judges to er.....judge the poetry. We will be asking all our poets onto the stage to recite their works themselves...'

'Oops, I wasn't expecting that,' said Hamish, hastily reviewing his poem.

'That way,' McVicars went on, 'there will be no anonymous nonsense to upset the judges and we'll see the culprits for ourselves..... And of course, we'll be able to listen to the beautiful poetry too.'

'So without further ado, please welcome the first contestant, Miss Allison Lansbury.'

There was a ripple of polite clapping. Allison hopped up the stairs and walked up to the mike.

'The purple-headed heather,' Allison began her poem with poise and grace. She had the crowd captured by her lilting voice and the last line about her immature true love was delivered with a venomous punch as she looked directly into George's eyes. Then she smiled sweetly and glanced across the faces of her audience, who burst into a spontaneous round of applause.

Next there were a couple of local girls reading their poems about porridge. An old lady followed, reciting a short ditty about her wee black Scottie dog. A couple of Japanese tourists took the stage after that but nobody could make out a word they said. The applause they received was as much for participation and good manners, as for style and quality.

More porridge poems followed. Poems about mountains and streams and a poem about sheep that raised an eyebrow or two.

Hamish withdrew his entry at this point, mumbling something about a sore throat, as he shoved his scrap of paper deep into the pocket of his shorts. The dirty vicar with the microphone looked slightly relieved, as the change of rules had the desired affect.

'Stage fright, I suspect,' whispered Allison.

'He's frightened alright,' said Kenny. 'Frightened of the response from old smelly McVicars. His poem started with the line 'There was a young chap from Madras, Who had an enormous.....'

'OK, Kenny! I get the picture,' she said jumping in before he could go too far.

'Please give a big Drumnadrochit welcome to....'

'You're on,' and Allison gave Kenny a dig in the ribs.

'....Kenny Roberts, Another contestant all the way from Little Pumpington.'

Kenny jumped up the steps and positively ran to the microphone. He was waving his paper in front of him and was beaming from ear to ear.

'There's a bit of a show-off about that boy,' said Allison. George grunted.

'Ahem,' said Kenny, clearing his throat before he began. *'Hey, diddle diddle,'* he read,
'The cat did a piddle,
All over the kitchen floor.
The little dog laughed,
To see such fun.
So the cat pee'd a little bit more.'
A few of the old men in the audience were chuckling. Children were laughing and pointing. 'He said pee, Mum.' And the general response was reasonably favourable considering his a poem about a cat making a mess in the kitchen. George felt proud for his friend, who taken a chance with a slightly risqué piece of poetry but Kenny had just about won over the audience.

'Eh, yes. That was......erm......' Reverend McVicars hesitated, '...different, shall we say.'

'Wait till they get a load of me,' said George under his breath.

'What's yours about, George?' asked Hamish quietly.

'Let's just say it's about poo,' smiled George wickedly.

'Ye mean, you've written your poem about a jobby?' gasped Hamish, wishing he'd went up on stage now.

'And next up is another young man from Little Pumpington and our final contestant of the day..... Mr George Hansen.' The minister clapped slowly, unsure what was about to follow.

George was laughing away, as he stepped up to the microphone and he hadn't even started reading his poem yet. This made the vicar more nervous. Allison definitely thought that was a bad sign.

'How's young Wordsworth doing?' asked Grandpa Jock, appearing from behind the crowd.

'He's about to start, Mr Jock' replied Kenny. 'You're just in time.'

'How's the porridge coming along, Mr Jock?'

'Oh smashing, Allison, all prepared,' he said. 'We're just ready to go for the final cook-off at four o'clock.'

'Shhh,' whispered Kenny, 'George is ready to start.'

On stage George was still grinning manically. In his hand was the little pocket note book he'd been scribbling in earlier. This was it....

'Jeremy the Jumping Jobby, By George Hansen,' said George proudly. One or two of the old dears in the audience gasped, Grandpa Jock sniggered and the vicar gulped. But there was no stopping George now...

'Once, there was a little boy,
I think we'll call him Robbie.
Who sat upon the toilet all day,
Playing his favourite hobby…
Jeremy sat,
In the tunnel so black
Ready to jump,
To start the attack.
Butt commander shouted,
'He's ready to blow!'
Jeremy tensed,
'Go, Go, Go!'
Jeremy jumped,
Out of the hole.
And down he splashed
Into the bowl.'

George looked up from his note book to see the crowd's reaction once they'd realised where Jeremy the Jobby had been sitting. Kinda obviously really, when you thought about it. He went on...

'The attack had begun.
The war had started.
And it all kicked off
When wee Robbie farted.
Jeremy dived,
To avoid the crush,
Reinforcements were coming
So he swam with the flush.
There was something going on
In that weird mind of Robbie's
Because he'd created
An army of jobbies.
Round the u-bend
Jeremy jumped.
Joined by more soldiers,
Each time Robbie pumped.
Jeremy the Jobby
Jumped into the sewer.
He met lots of old poo there,
And some that were newer.
The Poo Army was waiting
For a chief to take charge.
Jeremy's credentials?
Brown, smelly and large.'

All the children and most of the men were laughing by now. George had a hard time delivering the line 'Brown, smelly and large' with a straight face but he kept going.

'There were millions of poo there,
The sewer was packed
Waiting for a jobby
To lead the attack.
There were jobbies from Germany

And poo there from Spain.
They arrived at the airport,
Dumped out on a plane.
One jobby called Carlos,
Who came from Madrid,
Said, 'You cannot lead us'
'I must forbid."

George did his best to put on a Spanish accent at this point. How would a Spanish jobby talk, he thought?

"I've been a leader'
'Seence the day I was born'
'Look at my muscles'
'They're packed with sweetcorn'
But Jeremy argued,
'I'm the one born from Robbie'
'That makes me the best,'
'The world's number one jobby'
'I'm shiny and smelly,'
'I stink bad. Come on, sniff me.'
'And I'll lead this army.'
'Let's go, boys. Who's with me?'
The Army of Poo,
All joined Jeremy's side.
Six million poos deep,
Ten thousand poos wide.
'Come on poop, let's go!'
Jeremy did yell.
'We'll take over the world
With our God-awful smell.'
And the Army of Poo
Marched out onto the street,
But Juan shouted, 'Don't leesen,
'He doesn't know speet.'
Jeremy jumped out,

And the people yelled 'Yuck!'
But just at that moment
He was hit by a truck!
The truck started skidding,
What else could it do?
The wheels had no grip,
On the river of poo.
Cars started crashing,
Bumpers were shattered.
In the multi-car pile-up,
The jobbies were splattered.
From the sewer, whispered Carlos,
'His plan was absurd.'
'Why did they leesen,'
'To that Jeremy turd?'
Bang, bang, bang, went the door.
'Hurry up in there, Robbie'
'Don't tell me you're sitting there,'
'Dreaming of jobby!"

'The end,' shouted George triumphantly. The children started first, led by Hamish, clapping and cheering their appreciation but the vicar just held his head in his hands. Elderly men in the audience glanced across the elderly women first and saw that some of the older ladies had to wave fans or newspapers in front of their faces to cool down. Had George over-stepped the mark? The old geezers decided not to clap.

Realising that no one else was joining in, the children's applause dropped to a ripple and then the clapping became slow and methodical. George gulped and took a quick bow. His bravado and confidence were leaving far quicker than they'd arrived.

To silence, George left the stage and the tweed-jacketed reverend picked up the microphone.

'Well, er...thank you young Mr....er... Hansen.' He read George's name from a piece of card in his hand. 'That was ahem... a bit.....er quite unique, shall we say. I hope we don't hear a poem as special as that for quite a while. Now, the judges will take a little time to reach their decision and the winner will be announced at 6 o'clock, after the porridge tastings. See you back here then.'

'Well, I thought it was brilliant,' said Grandpa Jock. 'I nearly lost my false teeth laughing.'

'Yeah, George, it was great,' said Kenny joining in.

'You'll have to come back next year, George. I think that your poem freaked out some of the stuffier residents,' added Hamish.

'Don't look so down, George,' said Allison, putting her hand on his shoulder. 'They're very religious, straight-laced people up here. Everybody goes to church on Sunday and they are very strict about it. A poem about a jumping jobby was probably a bit of a shock.'

George shrugged his shoulder to shake off Allison's hand. Why was he being such a grump...even he wasn't so sure?

'Anyway, let's go Allison,' said Grandpa Jock, spinning on his old heels, 'We've got to get going for the final part of the porridge making contest.' And the two of them headed for the big marquee through the dispersing crowd.

'Come on, George. Don't feel so bad,' urged Kenny. 'You heard what the other entries were like...all poems about flowers and porridge. Allison's right. A poem about jobbies was way too shocking for the locals.'

'Aye, George, and that was far worse than Angus' attempt last year,' nodded Hamish. 'And by worse, I mean better.'

Chapter 11 – The Judging

George, Kenny and Hamish fought their way into the big marquee as the porridge judging was about to take place. Porridge doesn't take long to make, only around thirty minutes or so, but for the speciality competitors it's the preparation they put into it that makes all the difference.

Pots were steaming, kettles were bubbling and chefs were running around, waving spatulas above their heads and shouting obscenities at each other.

In the middle of the tent, and George hadn't noticed before because he was moping around feeling sorry for himself, was a large central platform, much bigger than the poetry stage. On this platform were a long trestle table and three chairs. Sitting on the table were several large trophies and a number of medals. And in the centre of the table stood a large golden cooking pot with a golden rolling pin in it.

'That's the Golden Spurtle trophy,' said Hamish with awe in his voice.

'Those must be for the winners,' Kenny pointed out, nodding over to the table.

'You think?!' grumbled George, sarcastically.

'You know, George, you can be a right miserable git sometimes.' replied Kenny. 'You might be annoyed with Allison for stealing your grandpa's attention, but don't take it out on me.' And he stormed off towards Grandpa Jock's cooking table. Hamish just shrugged, not sure which direction to go off in.

George couldn't describe his feelings. He'd been angry with Grandpa Jock when he made Allison his number one assistant cook. Grandpa Jock has trusted Allison with the shopping for a few special ingredients before they left Little Pumpington; that was his job! Why hadn't his grandpa asked him to do the shopping?

And wasn't Allison just acting up as the little chef; she was practically rubbing George's nose in it, running around, playing at being Grandpa's little helper. Wasn't she? Now Kenny was taking her side too. What was wrong with these people? What was wrong with George?

'We're still OK to go out on the boat tonight, right?' asked Hamish, a little lost.

'Yeah, I'm sure we are. My grandpa was quite excited about the idea when we told him,' replied George, trying to pick his mood up.

Before they could say anything else, Laird Baird strode up onto the stage. He was followed by two elderly ladies, who were dressed in their fanciest outfits. One wore a silk blouse and cardigan and practically all of her jewellery; the other wore a pale blue matching skirt and cashmere jacket. She had a big pearl necklace around her neck and her hair was pulled tight into a bun. The World Porridge Championships was a big day for the judges too, so they had to look their best.

'There's Laird Baird,' whispered Hamish, pointing. 'And she's Old Miss McParvis, who wet herself last year. The other lady in the blue is the Sunday school teacher, Miss Mackinnon. She's not quite right in the head. We call her Mad Mackinnon. She won't even let you go to the toilet when you're bursting.'

'Each of the teams has three minutes to present their speciality porridge to the judges,' Hamish continued. 'The judges assess colour, consistency, presentation and taste. It's all about the blending and the harmony of the flavours.'

Laird Baird had picked up the microphone and had welcomed all the chefs and visitors to the competition.

'So without further ado,' Laird Baird announced. 'May we have the first contestant please? I give you the reigning world champions, Mexico, with their version of crispy porridge nachos, thistle salsa with a turnip guacamole.'

'Oh aye, that's smart, very cunning indeed,' said Hamish, tapping the side of his nose. 'They've mixed Scottish and Mexican flavours. Porridge fusion, man!'

The judges picked up little spoons from the table and sampled the Mexican's creation. Their main bowl had been decorated with red chillies and a pair of flags, one Scottish, one Mexican standing up in the centre of the porridge. The judges tasted the dish, and then crowded their heads down together in whispered conversation.

'Next, the English entry, Heston Bloomingheck with his renowned Snail Porridge,' the announcer shouted, and a tall bald man with glasses walked up onto the stage holding a bowl shaped like a large snail's shell.

'Snail porridge! That's not English,' yelled George. 'That's what the French eat.'

'Naw, George, shhht,' hissed Hamish. 'Mr Heston has been coming here for years with his weird and wonderful creations. He's always putting a British twist on worldwide foods. He's brilliant!'

George curled his lip up, seemingly unimpressed.

The English celebrity chef was soon followed by the Germans, the Spaniards and a host of other entries. George was watching the judges closely and so far, they didn't seem too impressed. During several tastings, George thought he saw the judges actually gag. Mad Miss Mackinnon, sitting prim and proper in her cashmere suit, had even spat a mouthful of porridge into her handbag, when she thought no one was looking.

'It's not going too well, then,' suggested George, when Laird Baird obviously spat his mouthful back into the bowl, not caring who was watching.

'This is awfy strange,' said Hamish, shaking his head.

69

'They judges are usually stuffing their faces and practically licking the bowls clean by now. There's something suspicious going on.'

'Just the Americans and my Grandpa Jock left,' whispered George, pointing to the bottom of the stage, where the three scientists stood, carrying a pseudo space-age contraption with smoke flowing up and over the edges of the metal bowl. The bottom of the bowl had tripod feet so it looked like a 1950's style space rocket.

Behind them, Grandpa Jock was waiting patiently, holding a pouring jug and a long thin plastic pencil. Allison was carrying what looked like a large, round, white Xmas pudding on a plate. The plate was decorated with a garland of thistles.

The scientists stepped up to the platform and placed their plate of porridge in the middle of the table. The judges nodded their heads with appreciation at the culinary presentation. They picked up their spoons and dipped them into the mixture, which was a speckled blue colour.

'Looks like space food,' whispered Hamish. The crowd stared on intently.

As the judges rolled the porridge around their mouths, George could hear little clicking noises, cracks and pops. The judges raised their eyebrows and looked pleasantly surprised by the sensation.

Of course, thought George. Popping Space Porridge! That's the blue sugary granules they were mixing up in the jar, like that sweety dust stuff that explodes on your tongue as it dissolves.

George watched as the little pops began to get bigger inside the judges' mouths. Their eyes began to bulge as the cracks and snaps got louder and louder. Laird Baird stood up and stuck his tongue out. It was bright blue and George could see that it was covered in exploding little crystals.

The tiny rocks would burst with a small bang and pieces of 'moon rock' were sprayed over the crowd.

Miss Mackinnon was having a hard time just holding her false teeth in place whilst the other lady judge, Old Miss McParvis had porridge dripping out from the side of her mouth, as sugary granules were still bursting at the back of her throat.

The leading scientist, who presented the bowl onto the table, stared in horror at the mouth-popping judging panel. This was not the reaction he'd been hoping for. He snatched up a spoon to taste the blue, smoking concoction and was quickly joined by his companions.

Within seconds, the scientist's head was almost blown off as the little rocks began to explode ferociously. This porridge was closer to nitro-glycerine than confectionary.

'Sthabotath!' shouted science geek, his tongue hanging limply out the corner of his mouth, his glasses dangling off one ear. "Sthabotath!"

'Yeth, yeth,' shouted the other two, scraping at their tongues. 'Thomebody'th thpiked our porridth!'

'Yes, indeed,' cried Old Miss McParvis, finally regaining some composure. 'I'm quite inclined to agree with these gentlemen. This porridge has been sabotaged.'

Chapter 12 – Sabotage!

There was a gasp from the audience and a disbelieving murmur ran round the tent. Sabotage? Could this porridge really have been tampered with and who would want to taint the taste? A scandal like this could rock Drumnadrochit for years.

'Silence, ladies and gentlemen,' Laird Baird was standing up and wiping the porridge from his beard with a napkin.

'I must agree with Miss McParvis. I am of the belief that almost all the dishes that we've sampled today have been sabotaged. Too much salt, too much mustard, too much spice, too much garlic and in the case of this exploding monstrosity, too much dynamite. Allow us to confer on the matter.'

Over at the corner of the stage, ready to present his dish Grandpa Jock looked concerned and confused. He tucked the white plastic tube into his shirt pocket, transferred the sauce jug over to his left hand and took a lump of porridge from the big ball on the plate. He chewed it, he tasted and finally, he swallowed it.

Allison looked up at him nervously. He nodded to her confidently, his porridge pudding tasted fine. It didn't taste bad and certainly hadn't been tampered with.

By the exit, Team American, with exploding space rocks still popping on their blue tongues, were storming out of the tent in disgust, dragging their gas cylinders and pressure pots with them.

'They don't look happy, do they?' pointed George to the disappearing geek team.

Grandpa Jock stared across at George and George shrugged his shoulders. Hamish nudged him 'They've made a decision.'

The large judge took the microphone from the stand.

'It is the view of the judging panel,' he began. 'That the quality of entries, by such esteemed competitors and passionate porridge purists from around the world, have been so bad this year that we can only conclude that a dire plot has been undertaken to spoil, taint and contaminate every entry so far.'

The crowd began to mutter loudly. The Laird lifted his hand and raised his voice to speak over the rumblings of discontent.

'There can be only one reason for such interference and incapacitation, 'the judge boomed. 'And that is to allow one competitor to cheat, defraud and swindle their way to the title of the World Porridge Champion and the coveted trophy, the Golden Spurtle.'

The angry crowd had started booing and hissing, some of them throwing their programs at the stage and a few were shouting 'Cheat! and 'Find them and hang them!'

'This could get ugly,' whispered Hamish, his eyes scanning the crowd behind them.

'Settle down, ladies and gentlemen,' Laird Baird said with calm authority, regaining some order. 'The judges have decided that it is only fair that we will sample the final dish before agreeing on our next course of action.'

Grandpa Jock visibly gulped. He'd tasted his porridge; it was fine. In fact, it was better than fine, it was one of the most delicious, creamy, smooth porridges he'd ever made. But what would the audience think if his porridge was so scrumptious and every other team had their recipe meddled with? It would be carnage.

'Would The Jock Squad please step forward with their creation, Heather-Honeyed Haggis Porridge with a Whisky-Caramel and Raisin Sauce,' announced the Laird.

Grandpa Jock crept onto the stage, Allison behind him. The tray looked magnificent, with the porridge shaped into a large ball surrounding the honey haggis centre and the garland of thistles around the plate. The dish oozed Scottish-ness and the mob crowded forward, peering up to see the final, untasted entry.

The colour had drained from Grandpa Jock's face as he poured the creamy contents of his little jug over the top of the porridge. The delicate whisky sauce drizzled over the large round pudding and the juicy raisins slipped across the surface.

The audience were hushed. Grandpa Jock had been hoping to impress the judges with his presentation but now he was only hoping to make it out of the marquee alive. He slipped the white plastic tube from his pocket; George could see it closer now. It wasn't a pencil; it was a gas lighter.

Grandpa Jock clicked down on the trigger and small orange flare appeared. He pointed it towards the porridge and the whisky sauce went up in a puff of blue flame. The alcohol in the whisky blazed brightly and the appreciative 'ooh's' and 'aah's' Grandpa Jock had been hoping to hear had been replaced by a suspicious silence.

As the flames died down, each of the judges picked up their spoons again. They eyed the porridge carefully before slipping a small piece into their mouths.

They chewed it slowly, and then swallowed. It was pleasant enough. Nice whisky warmth from the sauce, creamy, tasty porridge itself. Laird Baird nodded in satisfaction. Miss Mackinnon smiled sweetly. The crowd growled.

The three judges dug their spoons in again for a second taste. Beneath the layer of porridge was the honeyed-haggis centre, which looked plump and juicy. Their spoons were bursting as they shovelled them into their mouths.

Moans of pleasure came from the judges mouths. Groans

of discontentment came from the crowd. Laird Baird, Old Miss McParvis and Mad Miss Mackinnon were delighting in the rich sweetness of the honey and the smooth creaminess of the porridge. The audience were thinking they'd found the saboteurs.

Now to taste this whisky cream sauce properly, thought all three of the judges at exactly the same moment. This was the best porridge they'd tasted all day and they weren't about to stop now. The raisins in the sauce looked plump, moist and bursting with flavour. Grandpa Jock gulped again. His delight at the judges enjoying his food was now totally overwhelmed by his fear that the agitated audience would think him the saboteur. Miss McParvis was first to take a huge mouthful.

Laird Baird swallowed his spoonful next and chewed on the juicy fruit. Miss Mackinnon was scooping out more haggis and mixing it with the raisins and cream. She guzzled it down with far less decorum that she pretended she had.

Old Miss McParvis was first to baulk. A mouthful of sick spewed up into her throat and she put her hand over her mouth. It splattered everywhere and little bits of vomit dribbled out between her fingers. Laird Baird coughed. Then he choked. Then he began spitting out the raisins onto the floor with gagging hack.

Mad Miss Mackinnon had turned a delicate shade of green. She'd swallowed her mouthful of haggis, porridge and raisins in one greedy gulp and now the food was starting to make its way back up again as soon as it hit her stomach. But it was too late. She opened her mouth and sprayed the crowd with torrents of projectile vomit.

In desperation, Miss Mackinnon grabbed her handbag and buried her face in it. The crowd stepped backwards and winced at the gut-twisting wrenches that poured from the old lady with her head in a bag.

'Rabbits ....aherrrgh,' coughed Laird Baird again, with chunks of regurgitated porridge stuck in his beard. He cleared his throat and took a sip of water from the desk. Then spewed again.

'The porridge sauce has rabbit poo in it!' he declared.

'You mean, we're eating bunny jobby!' squealed Miss McParvis, with another wretch. Miss Mackinnon still had her face in her bag.

The crowd groaned in unison at the yucky thought. George and Hamish chuckled together. George turned and saw Kenny sniggering too.

'Well, that wasn't in the recipe,' argued Grandpa Jock, to no one in particular. Allison's face was absolutely chalk-white. She'd been in charge of the sauce and George felt a little sorry for her.

'No, no, it's alright, Jock,' the Laird had stood up and wiped his beard with a napkin. 'Your porridge has been sabotaged too.' He turned and nodded to the other judges.

'Ladies and gentlemen, a shocking scandal has taken place today and the good name of the World Porridge Championships has been dragged down into the sewer.' Laird Baird shook his head sadly.

'An investigation will begin immediately. The championships will recommence tomorrow, under the tightest security!'

And then Mad Miss Mackinnon barfed loudly into her handbag again.

Chapter 13 – Tests Confirmed

The three scientists squeezed through the bulkhead hatch and headed single file along the narrow corridor. The door clanged behind them and their boots clunked on the metal gangway.

The research cabin was cramped and compact. The desk in the corner was surrounded by banks of computer screens, seismic echo-sound recorders and sonar scan TV monitors.

The three men in white lab coats pressed inside and each moved to a different station.

'Hydrophone sensors all clear, professor,' said the thinnest scientist with the thickest glasses.

This was Doctor Peewee Peterson, the eminent geologist and hydrologist who spent his entire career studying the interaction of rocks, groundwater movement and theoretical saturated, subsurface hydrogeology (basically, just a swanky name for studying puddles).

Although he'd been married three times, his wives didn't want to remain married to him for too long, and Peewee was first to admit that he was, possibly, the most boring scientist in the world. Although he had an IQ of 207 (the average is about 100 and genius level starts at 160) he spent most of his adult life looking at rocks.

Next to report in was Commander Chuck Choppers, aquamarine biologist and former US Navy Oceanographer. Chuck was much taller than Peewee but he also wore thick glasses, one leg of which was held together with sticky tape. He kept a row of plastic ballpoint pens in the top pocket of his lab coat, just because you never knew when you'd need to take notes.

His real name was Charles but his father had called him Chuck his whole life, hoping to toughen him up. His dad was a US Navy Seal; one of the roughest men ever to come out of Texas and he wanted a rock hard, macho man for a son. When young Charles started keeping tadpoles and called them names like Fifi, Trixy and Little Miss Taddy PeePee, his strict father swiftly packed him off to military school so fast his tadpoles hadn't time to grow legs.

At military school, Chuck learnt to shoot machine guns, play with explosives, drive tanks, sail submarines and even fly helicopters but he wasn't interested in developing his muscles like the other camp cadets. Chuck Choppers was only interested in developing his mind so instead of being in the gym all the time, he read books and studied for his exams. He was probably the skinniest, geekiest, highly trained, combat killing machine the world had ever seen.

Except the world hadn't really seen Chuck Choppers. He spent all his time studying lung-fish, conger eels and sea urchins.

'Nothing to report on the seismic data sheets, professor,' squeaked Chuck Choppers, his true persona far removed from the tough namesake his daddy wanted. 'Although surface level reports show a further rise in water levels by 0.03 centimetres in the last six hours.'

Professor Marmaduke Spicer nodded quietly. Professor Spicer, or Marmy to his friends, was in charge of this vehicle, the financial budget and the whole expedition. A lover of porridge, a professor of palaeontology and cryptozoology and the biggest ever brain to walk out of Harvard University; Marmaduke Spicer had made his fortune as a big, and not so big game hunter. His latest book, a worldwide bestseller, detailed the life of the hairy Yeti Crab of South Pacific, which uses the hairs on its pincers to detoxify minerals from the water flowing from the hydrothermal, lava vents where the crab lives. Then it eats its own poo!

Professor Spicer was only 38 years old and still very young to be a professor but his genius and foresight into the minds of prehistoric animals, fish and dinosaurs gave him an uncanny and almost supernatural perception of the lives of extinct creatures. His textbooks were legendary; his seminars were sold-out months in advance and his attentions had been attracted to the strange happenings in the overflowing lochs of Scotland and the fast drying lakes of England. This phenomenon had not been witnessed in over 10,000 years and Professor Marmaduke Spicer had brought together a crack team of experts to help him solve the mystery.

And make some good porridge at the same time.

Spicer took on board the information for a second, and then said quietly, 'So where is the additional liquid coming from? It hasn't rained in weeks and lochs do not fill up by themselves.'

This was Peewee Peterson's field of expertise. Showing off wasn't his style but he wanted to prove to Professor Spice that he'd chosen the right man for the job.

Peterson began. 'The study of the interaction between groundwater movement and geology can be quite complex, sir. Groundwater does not always flow down-hill underground.'

Peterson waited for some acknowledgement. None came, so he carried on. 'Subsurface water does not follow the surface topography. Water follows pressure gradients that flow from high pressure to low pressure environments, often following undersea fractures and conduits in circuitous paths...'

'Speak gosh-darn English, you numbskull!' yelled the professor. 'I have an IQ of 229 and I have no idea what you just said. Again!'

'Er...underground, fresh water is s-s-sometimes pushed

upwards by force and doesn't necessarily flow downwards and it flows in b-b-big circles in tidal currents,' stammered Peewee Peterson.

'Professor, you might want to take a look at this,' Chuck Choppers was pointing at the data screen with a bar graph growing green, then red. 'The saline levels of the water have risen 0.02% in the same time period, sir!'

'The water is getting saltier? How?' Marmaduke Spicer closed his eyes, thinking over the problem.

'No just salty, sir. More acidic too.'

Acid, in Loch Ness? Where was it coming from? Professor Marmaduke had a lot to consider.

Chapter 14 - And The Winner Is....

The crowd in the marquee had begun to disperse quietly, having realised that Grandpa Jock wasn't to blame for sabotaging anybody's porridge. One or two of them looked a little disappointed.

Grandpa Jock, Kenny and Allison walked across to where George and Hamish were standing. Kenny was never one to hold a grudge so he was first to speak.

'Bit of a close one, eh,' he said, raising his eyebrows.

'Aye, you're not wrong there, laddie.' Grandpa Jock was wiping his sweaty brow. 'I thought for one minute we'd be in big trouble if our porridge was uncontaminated. Would've looked a bit suspicious.'

'Well, thank goodness for rabbit poo, really,' said George, grinning. 'And who was responsible for the cream sauce?'

'That was me,' replied Allison.

'Oh right then,' and George left the observation hanging in the air.

'What are you suggesting, Gorgeous?' Allison snapped.

Now George wasn't exactly gorgeous, far from it. If he was Mr Potato-Head then he would've been put together by a blindfolded orang-utan in a bag. Some mean kids at school might occasionally tease him about his one ear bigger than the other, or his right eye higher than the left but he never expected to hear it from his friends. Allison really wasn't going to take that dig lying down.

'Are you saying I wrecked our own sauce, George? Why would I do that, eh?'

'That's not what I was suggesting,' shrugged George. 'I just think you could've been a bit more carefully, keeping your eye on it, that's all.'

'Why, you cheeky...' Allison was raging now. 'I didn't even think for one minute that you'd be petty enough to spoil our porridge but the way you've been acting recently George, with your juvenile jealousy and small-minded resentment.....'

'Right, stop!' declared Grandpa Jock, taking charge and acting like a proper adult for a change. 'George didn't tamper with the porridge, ours or anybody else's. And Allison, you did a fine job with the sauce.'

Tempers were still frayed and the atmosphere was tense.

'Somebody was serious about sabotaging all the dishes. Some professional, someone who knew what they were doing so let's not start fighting amongst ourselves,' said Grandpa Jock, lowering his voice slowly, to calm everyone down. Deep breaths were taken slowly. Grandpa Jock paused.

'OK, that's better,' he said softly. 'Now, why don't we go out to the poetry competition to see who the winners were?'

Allison was first to make a move to the exit, her head held up haughtily and eyes facing straight forward. George didn't want to look at her anyway, so he thrust his hands deep into his pockets and shuffled out of the tent beside his Grandpa Jock.

'What is it with those two?' asked Hamish, with wide-eyed amazement.

'I think one of them fancies the other one,' chuckled Kenny. 'But neither of them wants to admit it.'

*

The crowd from the porridge marquee had all made their way out to the poetry stand to hear the results of, at least, one competition that day. Well, it was a pretty rubbish fair anyway, thought George, so there wasn't a lot else left to do, unless you wanted to buy a doll with a knitted dress to cover toilet rolls with.

Reverend McVicars was standing on the stage with a handful of scrap paper between his fingers. Around his wrist hung three medals and he held a small gold trophy in his left hand.

'Get on with it!' shouted a voice from the crowd, as the sense of frustration rippled below the surface.

'Er, yes, yes, er thank you,' the vicar stuttered. 'It gives me great pleasure to announce the winners of the Drumnadrochit Poetry Competition. The standard has been quite remarkable this year, with er...one or two minor exceptions, and it was a difficult choice for the judges to make. Finally, however, we have managed to reach an overall majority decision which....'

'Hurry up!' yelled a voice from the back. The unease, which had been sparked by the postponement of the porridge competition, was now permeating through the whole crowd. The judge wasn't about to add fuel to the flames.

'It'll be yours, mate,' said George, nudging Kenny in the ribs, reaffirming his friendship. 'Short and sweet. Nice.'

'Nah, man,' replied Kenny. 'Yours was epic! I'd definitely vote for Jeremy the Jumping Jobby.'

'Let's hope the hearts and flowers rubbish doesn't win,' growled George.

'Oh come on, mate. Don't spoil it.' Kenny didn't want to take sides but George was still festering. Allison was staring straight at the stage so she didn't appear to want to make the first move either.

'You're a pair of stubborn tubes, so ye are,' said Hamish.

'....and the winner of the 'Highly Recommended' prize in the Porridge, Pets and Places category goes to......' George thought the vicar should've had a drum roll at this point. 'Wee Moira McMoran, with the special rendition of her poem 'My Parrot Polly Loves Porridge. Let's give it up for wee Moira.'

Finally getting to see some prizes awarded, the crowd burst into an enormous show of appreciation and pent-up relief, clapping, cheering and hollering. A little red haired girl with bunches in her hair and skin covered with freckles jumped onto the stage and bowed to let the judge slip the ribbon around her neck. She puffed out her chest to show off the silver medal.

'We like to see a local winner,' admitted Hamish, slapping his hands together loudly.

'And moving onto the next prize,' announced the old church-man. 'We have the winner of the 'Highly Recommended' award for the Romance and Nature category, the beautiful, heart-wrenching tale of unrequited love by.....'

'He'd better hurry up,' whispered George to both Kenny and Hamish. 'The crowd won't take much more of this.'

'Allison Lansbury from Little Pumpington!' Kenny, Hamish and the rest of the crowd whooped and cheered. Allison bowed her head to accept her medal, trying to look both humble and grateful at the same time. She smiled at Kenny and Grandpa Jock as she stepped down from the stage. Strangely, George was busy tying his shoe laces at that moment.

'And finally, the winner of the overall grand prize in the Porridge Poetry competition goes to....'

This time Kenny, Hamish and few of the younger children did create a drum-roll effect by rapping their hands furiously on the stage. George held his breath.

'...Drumnadrochit's very own Dougal McSporran with his wonderful, heart-warming poem 'The Magnificent Man-eating Midges of Morar'.

With another local poetry champion collecting a prize, the crowd went mad. George thought that young Dougal bore a striking resemblance to the vicar presenting him with his

trophy and it took every fibre of his being not to shout 'Fix!'

In fact, off to the other side of the stage there seemed to be an entire clan of McSporrans standing, screaming and cheering. Mums, dads, uncles, aunties, brothers, sisters and cousins, they were all proud of their little winner.

George thought; it would be churlish to think that some family influence was a factor on the judges' decision. He knew Jeremy the Jumping Jobby was a classic, but had to accept that maybe it wasn't quite good enough to sway a partisan voting panel. George tried not to feel too bitter and Allison saw something in his eyes.

'Never mind, George,' she said, softening. 'I thought your poem was....er special and quite unique.'

'Huh, that's easy for you to say. You won a prize.'

Allison shrugged her shoulders and turned to Kenny. 'At least I tried,' she said and Kenny nodded reluctantly.

'Right, you lot,' shouted Grandpa Jock. 'We're on holiday, we're going monster hunting tonight and we're supposed to be having a blast....'

He lifted his leg, scrunched up his face and squeezed out the most enormous bottom burp of the holiday so far.

'Trump that!' he declared and George, Kenny, Allison and Hamish burst out laughing.

'Well, I'm relieved to hear it.'

Chapter 15 – Monster Hunting

It was past 9 o'clock in the evening but it was still light
when the five of them climbed in Hamish's rowing boat and
set off for the centre of Loch Ness. It was a sturdy craft;
four metres long with three benches in the middle and a
dirty tarpaulin sheet scrunched up and dumped in the stern
of the boat. George thought Hamish probably used that
sheet to cover the boat when it was moored.

George and Kenny had volunteered to do the rowing for
the first part of the journey; they'd never been on a rowing
boat before and wanted to test their boat captain skills.

After about 20 minutes, it became apparent that their
boating skills amounted to absolutely zero as they spent
the first 10 minutes pushing the boat off from shore, then
the rest of the time just rowing around in circles. Eventually
Hamish and Allison took over on the oars and some
progress was finally made.

Unfortunately, this didn't help with George's current
impression of Allison.

Grandpa Jock spotted the flicker of antagonism in
George's eyes and tried to deflect it.

'Row, row, row your boat,' he began to sing.

'Gently down the stream.'

'If you see a plesiosaur, don't forget to scream!'
Grandpa Jock squealed as loud as he could in the
girliest, high-pitched screeching voice he could manage.
Everybody laughed.

'Hamish,' chuckled George, 'Apart from last week, have
you ever seen anything on the loch before?'

'Naw, not really,' said Hamish, speaking in puffs, between
row strokes. 'I've heard all the stories, of course. Growing
up around here means you hear these stories every day;
then you repeat them and add to them. Pretty soon, you

can't remember what's real and what's fake.'

Hamish went on, 'Occasionally, if there's a genuine sighting the police will let off red flares into the sky as a signal to the locals. It would be good for tourism if someone could snap another photograph of a monster. It's been ages since the last one.'

'But it's a huge loch, isn't it?' said Kenny, staring around him at the huge expanse of water surrounding the boat.

'Aye, pretty big,' nodded Hamish with pride. 'By surface area it's the fourth biggest lake or loch in the British Isles,' he said sounding like a tour guide.

'Isn't it the deepest though?' added Grandpa Jock, eager to hear more.

'Aye, Mr Jock, it's the deepest alright,' Hamish eyebrows bobbed. 'They say it's almost as deep as Blackpool Tower and St Paul's Cathedral put together.'

'Deeper than Eiffel Tower?' asked George

'Not quite,' answered Hamish. 'But there's more water in Loch Ness than in all the lochs and lakes in Scotland, England and Wales combined.'

'No way!' shouted George, Kenny and Allison all together.

'It's true,' replied Hamish. 'This loch is so long and so deep that nobody really knows what lives in it.'

'You could fit the entire population of the world in Loch Ness ten times over,' announced Grandpa Jock. George was sure he'd been reading one of the travel brochures at the campsite.

'Aye, Mr Jock,' laughed Hamish, panting hard, 'that's nearly two thousand billion gallons of water.'

Grandpa Jock knew he'd been beaten. 'Aye, good one, lad. But we're still not getting very far. Let me take over on both oars. I'll show you how it's done.'

And he jumped up in the boat and hopped over to the centre, ushering Hamish and Allison back to the stern.

He plonked his bottom down onto the bench and his inflatable underpants squashed outwards at the sides under his weight.

'Steady, Grandpa! You're rocking the boat, man,' shouted George as he and Kenny gripped on.

Undeterred, Grandpa Jock grabbed an oar in each hand, dug them deep into the water and heaved hard. He quickly pulled into a rhythm and the boat began to skim across the surface of the water. He was certainly having more success than the other four rowers.

'Why is the water a murky brown colour,' asked George, splashing his hand into the water. 'It's like tea?'

'That's because of all the peaty soil around the loch,' said Hamish. Grandpa Jock had tried to answer that one, but was too out of breath. Hamish went on, 'Divers and even submarines can't really see anything down there.'

'What are those ruins over there? By the shoreline?' Allison was pointing to the west of the loch.

'That's Urquhart Castle,' replied Hamish. 'It's south of here that most of the sightings of the monster have been reported.'

After the initial burst of speed, the boat had slowed down considerably. Grandpa Jock had begun puffing and panting and his hair was sticking out wildly.

His face grimaced, he clenched his teeth and he dug his boots into the bottom of the boat. He tensed his muscles hard and pulled on the oars with all his strength. Stroke after stroke, Grandpa Jock dragged the boat through the water. Perhaps he was clenching too hard.

Pull. Parp!

George sat up. It was just a little squeaker but he knew what was coming next.

Puuulll. Parp!

Kenny and Allison heard it too that time.

Puuuuuuuullllll. Parp!

All four children were laughing now as the pressure in Grandpa Jock's stomach muscles squeezed out a wee fart at the end of each stroke. He pulled hard on the oars and as soon as the pressure was released, out popped a pump. His kilt wafted up with each blast too.

Puuuuuuuuuuuullllll. Par! Squidge!

'Right, that's it,' said Grandpa Jock, jumping up again. 'I've had enough. That one was too close for comfort, practically touching the cloth, so it was. And the paddles keep popping out of the water.'

'You just need to follow through with the oars, Mr Jock,' assured Hamish.

'Follow through?! I nearly followed through alright. Somebody else can take over, my piles are bothering me.'

'How long is Loch Ness anyway?' asked George, watching the water spread off in both directions, as the boat bobbed on the water.

Hamish replied, 'Roughly twenty three miles long. And about a mile and half wide, we're nearly in the middle.'

'OK,' said George dubiously. 'So, we've been rowing for about an hour and we've gone about half a mile. We're not covering much distance.'

Allison had got her breath back now, after the rowing. 'Yeah, Hamish, what's the plan? Is there a plan?'

'I suppose we're close enough to the centre of the loch now, so we can start the engine,' replied the young Scots lad.

'WE HAVE AN ENGINE?!' shouted Grandpa Jock, still red in the face. 'I nearly pooped my pants rowing this bloomin' thing and we have an engine?!'

'Well, I didn't want to make too much noise near the shore, you know, attract attention,' said Hamish, pulling the tarpaulin off an outboard motor at the rear of the boat. 'Plus, I didn't want to use too much petrol, too soon.'

'Aye, I might've guessed,' grunted Grandpa Jock. 'That's where us Scots get our reputation of being mean.'

'Not mean, Mr Jock, just careful.' And Hamish winked across at George as he pulled the oars into the boat.

Hamish set the propeller down gently into the water, with the rudder firmly clamped against the rear of the boat. He yanked hard on the pullcord and motor coughed into life. The boat chugged forward picking up speed steadily.

'Now we're talking!' said Grandpa Jock excitedly, clapping his hands together and forgetting about his near accident. The breeze was blowing his crown of orange hair around madly as the boat ploughed through the water.

'We'll head south, down to Cherry Island, wait a wee bit there and cruise back again.' Hamish was holding onto the rudder at the back whilst George, Allison and Kenny hung over the bow at the front.

'That's right,' gasped Kenny, 'you said before there was

only one island on Loch Ness.'

Angus replied, 'Yup, and it's not even a real island. It's called a crannog, that means man-made.'

'What?' Allison and George turned to stare at Hamish. George suddenly felt a little self-conscious being so close to Allison but she didn't seem to mind.

'Aye, it was built hundreds of years ago,' said Hamish, matter-of-factly. 'There used to be a small castle on it, used as a hunting lodge, but that's gone now.'

Kenny was staring out over the water straight ahead. He'd been at the front of the boat since he stopped rowing but hadn't seen so much of a ripple of a monster.

'There used to be another one nearby called Dog Island but that's submerged now that the water levels have risen so much,' Hamish went on. 'People think that's where the hunting dogs from the lodge were kept, years and years ago, when the island was above the surface.

George and Allison turned to the front of the boat again and stared out across Loch Ness. Allison glanced over at him and smiled. George wrinkled his nose and smiled back softly.

He wanted to talk to her but he felt awkward at feeling so stupidly jealous. So, she got on well with his Grandpa? She didn't know her grandparents; they'd died when she was very young. George felt a knot tightened in his stomach. Kenny was right; she wasn't competition, she was his friend.

George was mad at himself for behaving like an idiot. But he didn't know what to say, and he couldn't put his feelings into words. He'd have to wait for the right moment; maybe Allison would make the first move.

The little boat chugged onwards and the five of them sat in silence as the last light of the day disappeared behind the mountains.

Chapter 16 – In The Water

'What's that?!' shouted Kenny, pointing off into the distance.

'What? Where?' yelled everybody else.

'That black shape in the water. Can't you see it?'

George peered ahead screwing his eyes up and focussing on the black water line. 'I see it too. There's something out there.' Hamish smiled.

'Oh my goodness, it's huge,' shrieked Allison, as her eyes began to make out the tall, dark mass in front of the boat. It was approaching slowly....slowly.....slowly...

'Raaaarrrrrrrr!' growled Grandpa Jock.

'Aaaargh!' shrieked George, Allison and Kenny.

'What a fright, Grandpa!?' complained George. 'I nearly jumped out the boat then.'

'That'll teach you for laughing at me when I nearly pooped my pants,' giggled Grandpa Jock.

'What about the monster though?' Kenny was still pointing at the shape looming up in the blackness.

'That's Cherry Island, ya tube,' laughed Hamish. 'We're almost at the southern most tip of the loch. Fort Augustus is down there.'

'You mean that's the island?' George didn't believe his eyes anymore than Kenny did. The night was becoming darker now and murky shadows merged into each other.

BUMP!

The boat bounced a little.

'What was that?' screeched Kenny, who was normally calm but now, for some reason, was becoming more nervous by the minute.

'Be chilled, man,' hushed Hamish. 'We're probably brushing over the remains of Dog Island. It's submerged around here somewhere.'

'Are you sure? I would've said that was more of a 'bump' than a 'brush'.' Kenny was holding onto the edge of the boat, staring frantically at the surface of the water.

'Take it easy, Kenny,' said George, trying to reassure his friend.

'Take it easy? Take it blooming easy, he says!' Kenny was breathing hard. 'We're out here hunting giant prehistoric monsters in a little wooden boat and you want me to take it easy.'

'We don't know if there's a Loch Ness monster. We haven't seen anything yet,' asked Allison.

'Well, I've changed my mind. I don't want to see anything. I should've stayed on dry land.'

'Don't worry. We'll need to stay dry anyway; I've forgotten to bring the life jackets with us.' Hamish shrugged.

'It's okay,' reassured Grandpa Jock. 'No one's going in the water.'

BUMP!

The boat rocked to and fro, violently this time. Hamish cut the motor.

'See! See, definitely more 'bump' than 'brush' that time.'

'Did you see that? Off the starboard bow?' asked Allison, turning across to the side of the boat.

'Now she decides to get all nautical on us!' Kenny was close to freaking out. 'What's the starboard side?'

Grandpa Jock had stood up and stepped over the centre board. He put his hand on Kenny's shoulder.

'That's the starboard bow there, to the front right of the boat. 'Port' is the left hand side. Now, what did you see, girl?'

'There! Again!' Allison had turned to see if Grandpa Jock was looking in the right place.

'Yes! I saw it too,' George had seen something. Yes, he wanted to agree with Allison, to make amends, to support her but he really had seen something and he pointed to the water between the boat and the island.

A large, black scaly hide slipped below the water's surface and disappeared.

'I told you. I told you!' Hamish kept repeating. Kenny slunk deeper into the bottom of the boat. Allison sat alongside him. His face was chalk white and he'd stopped looking out at the water. He'd seen enough.

Three black humps rose silently from the water and slipped away again, this time on the far side of the boat. A mass of bubbles broke through the surface and gurgled on the water, followed by soft pink bobbing up then quickly back below. Another shape swam passed the boat, closer this time and several shadows circled in the depths but it was too dark to make out their true form.

Something small and dark broke through the water.

'A fin!' shouted Allison, jumping up and pointing out the back of the boat. She was standing on the bench near the bow. Kenny sat upright, his head nudging against Allison's legs.

A dark, diamond-shaped flipper glided across the water for a few seconds then disappeared below into the blackness.

BUMP!

The boat rocked.

Allison toppled backwards and plunged in the water.

'Allison! No!' cried George, reaching out to catch her. Grandpa Jock jumped forward and threw out his hand. Hamish grabbed an oar.

For a second Allison was visible on the surface. Hamish tried using the hook end of the oar to catch at her clothes but she sank away into the gloom.

'ALLISON!' shouted George, pulling off his jumper, ready to dive in. Hamish hauled him back by his arm.

'Ye can't, George. One in the water is bad enough. There are strong currents below the surface that can drag any swimmer into the deep.'

'That's why I have to save her!'

'No, he's right, lad. You can't go in,' said Grandpa Jock. 'Help me search with this oar.' They scanned the water for any sign of life. Allison was nowhere to be seen.

Kenny and Hamish worked frantically with one oar, Grandpa Jock and George with the other, pulling the paddles through the water hoping to snag the hook on Allison's clothes or something, anything. The water was black and murky.

Instinctively George turned.

'There she is!' he screamed.

About ten metres behind the boat, George could see Allison's hand just breaking the surface, reaching upwards.

'Something's dragging her,' Grandpa Jock whispered in disbelief.

'Come on, turn the boat. Turn the boat!' George began thrashing at the water with his hands. Hamish and Grandpa dug the oars into the water and the boat slowly edged around.

'She's going under again,' shouted Kenny, pulling at the water with George.

Allison's hand slipped from view into the blackness once more.

In the few seconds that it took until the boat reached the spot, Allison had disappeared. There was no trace, no bubbles or not even a shadow below the water.

Grandpa Jock and Hamish plunged the oars as deep as they dared but the loch held onto its secrets.

Allison was gone.

To be continued...

To be continued...

Follow the exciting conclusion in
Gorgeous George and the Unidentified, Unsinkable
Underpants Part 2

Gorgeous George
...and the Unidentified, Unsinkable Underpants
Part 2!
"IT'S UNDERPANTASTIC!" Says Charlie Higson from the Fast Show and author of 'The Enemy'
by
Stuart Reid
illustrated by John Pender

Don't Miss the Next Exciting Instalment of Gorgeous George and the Unidentified Unsinkable Underpants Is there really a Loch Ness Monster? What was it that bumped into the boat? Will Allison survive?

And who sabotaged all the porridge dishes? And will Grandpa Jock be able to 'hold it in' before he can get to the toilet the next time?

The water levels in Loch Ness continue to rise, whilst the drought goes on in England and the greatest scientific geeks in the known universe seem to be unable to solve the problem. George, Kenny and Grandpa Jock may need to lend a hand but only if Grandpa Jock can adjust the whoopee cushions that are sewn into his pants.

Will it ever occur to Grandpa Jock that, if there really is a Loch Ness Monster and the monster widdles in the water, then he just washed his dishes in wee-wee?

There's more than a few things hidden beneath the surface of Loch Ness and that's nothing compared to what's beneath the mountainside.

There's another competition as George and Kenny go head-to-head to prove their manhood. Whatever they're getting up to, it's guaranteed to be messy.

And find out if there is any truth in the rumour that eating too much asparagus turns your wee green!

Gorgeous George and the Unidentified Unsinkable Underpants Part 2

Chapter 17 – Drowning

Silence engulfed the small boat. The loch was still and the water was flat.

There was no moon but the sky was filled with an ocean of stars. They sparkled overhead and danced in the tiny ripples that lapped off the hull.

George sat in the well of the boat with his head in his hands. He sobbed quietly.

Kenny and Hamish were at the stern, sitting either side of the motor. They stared ahead, their eyes filled with tears, their minds filled with a shocking numbness of disbelief and anguish.

Grandpa Jock held onto the sides as he stared into the water. He'd been standing there, searching for thirty minutes. Allison had been under the water a long time.

'I'm sorry, lad,' he said quietly. 'It's no use. She's gone.'

'No, no. She can't be,' cried George, his eyes red, tears streaming down his cheeks.

'But her hand?' said Kenny. 'It was so still. She wasn't struggling or splashing. It was like she was waving and it just slipped into the water.'

'I'm sorry, boys' Grandpa Jock said again. 'That's what happens when water enters the lungs. The body stops fighting. It's not like the movies; someone who's drowning won't even be able to cry for help. It's called an instinctive drowning response; she wouldn't even be able to kick her legs.'

'But she can't be gone, Grandpa. I didn't tell her I was sorry,' George buried his head into his elbow. Tears flowed and he gasped for air between sobs.

'I'm so sorry, George.'

George wanted to turn back time; to take back the anger and jealousy he'd shown towards Allison. He felt guilty he was still alive and Allison wasn't. Why had they come to Loch Ness? Why had they come out on a stupid boat?

'We'll have to head into shore and report this to the police,' sighed Grandpa Jock. 'And they'll have to tell her parents too.' Hamish nodded and started to pull the chord. Grandpa Jock shook his head.

'Don't start the engine, lad. I couldn't bare the noise,' said Grandpa Jock softly as he rubbed his eyes. 'Anyway, we're close enough to row to shore.'

Grandpa Jock dipped the oars into the water and pulled back on them. Kenny sat still and silent. George had stopped crying and was breathing heavily.

Breathing. He was lucky to be breathing, he thought. Allison wasn't breathing. The pain in his chest clawed at his heart and tugged a knot from his stomach.

George thought about her death. He could think of nothing else. A cold, silent death, forcing air from her lungs and suffocating her beneath the water.

'Why? Why did she have to die?' shouted George, to no one in particular. 'Why couldn't I have said sorry sooner?'

'George, don't punish yourself. It's not your fault,' said Kenny, reaching out to his friend.

George snapped. 'I know it's not my fault! You butted her with your head when you jumped. You probably knocked her into the water yourself!'

'That's not what happened, George. It was an accident,' said Hamish, trying to defuse the situation.

'AND YOU! Coming out here without life jackets! In your stupid little boat. You're just as much to blame!' George was bright red in the face as he vented his anger. 'You're as much to blame as me!'

Hamish just bowed his head and said nothing. George was angrier with himself but just wanted to lash out, hoping to release the pain inside him. It didn't make him feel better though. He felt worse. He was hurting his friends now, trying to push out his own guilt as he knew his heart was breaking in a way he could never have imagined.

Grandpa Jock tucked the oars inside the boat, stepped over the centre board and sat down beside George. He put his arm around his grandson's shoulder and held him.

The rowing boat gently bumped up against the shoreline and bobbed there with each soft ripple of wave. Nobody wanted to move.

To be continued...

About the author, Stuart Reid

Stuart Reid is 48 years old, going on 10.

Throughout his early life he was dedicated to being immature, having fun and getting into trouble. After scoring a goal in the playground Stuart was known to celebrate by kissing lollypop ladies.

He is allergic to ties; blaming them for stifling the blood flow to his imagination throughout his twenties and thirties. After turning up at the wrong college, Stuart was forced to spend the next 25 years being boring, professional and corporate. His fun-loving attitude was further suppressed by the weight of career responsibility, as a business manager in the retail and hospitality industries in the UK and Dubai.

Stuart is one of the busiest authors in Britain, performing daily at schools, libraries, book stores and festivals with his book event Reading Rocks! He has appeared at over 950 schools and has performed to over 200,000 children. In 2015 Stuart was invited to tour overseas, with visits to schools in Ireland, Dubai and Abu Dhabi, performing for 120 princes at the Royal Rashid School For Boys.

He has performed his energetic and exciting book readings at the Edinburgh Fringe Festival, has been featured on national television, radio and countless newspapers and magazines. He won the Forward National Literature Silver Seal in 2012 for his debut novel, Gorgeous George and the Giant Geriatric Generator and was recently presented with the Enterprise in Education Champion Award by Falkirk Council.

Stuart has been married for over twenty years. He has two children, a superman outfit and a spiky haircut.

About the illustrator, John Pender

John is 36 and currently lives in Grangemouth with his wife Angela and their young son, Lucas, aged 4.

Working from his offices in Glasgow, John has been a professional graphic designer and illustrator since he was 18 years old, contracted to create illustrations, artwork and digital logos for businesses around the world, along with a host of individual commissions of varying degrees.

Being a comic book lover since the age of 4, illustration is his true passion, doodling everything from the likes of Transformers, to Danger Mouse to Spider-man and Batman in pursuit of honing his skills over the years.

As well as cartoon and comic book art, John is also an accomplished digital artist, specialising in a more realistic form of art for this medium, and draws his inspiration from acclaimed names such as Charlie Adlard, famous for The Walking Dead graphic novels, Glenn Fabry from the Preacher series, as well as the renowned Dan Luvisi, Leinil Yu, Steve McNiven and Gary Frank.

John has been married to Angela for 6 years and he describes his wife as his 'source of inspiration, positivity and motivation for life.' John enjoys the relaxation and stress-relief that family life can bring.

Photography is another of John's pleasures, and has established a loyal and enthusiastic following on Instagram.

The Gorgeous George Books

Gorgeous George and the Giant Geriatric Generator
The first Gorgeous George Adventure
Bogies, baddies, bagpipes and burps!
Farting, false teeth and fun!
Kindle: http://goo.gl/tXB7x4

Gorgeous George and the ZigZag Zit-faced Zombies

Sneezing, sniffing, snogging and snots. Zombies, zebras and zits!

**Gorgeous George and the Unidentified
Unsinkable Underpants Part 1**

Poo, plesiosaurs, porridge, pants! Monsters, mayhem & muck!

**Gorgeous George and the Unidentified
Unsinkable Underpants Part 2**

More monsters, more mayhem and more muck.
And pot-loads of porridge, poo, pumps and pants!

Gorgeous George and the Jumbo Jobby Juicer

Burgers, bottoms, baddies and burps.
Power pink, pumping and poop!

www.stuart-reid.com

For Gorgeous George T-Shirts, Cups, Bags, Notepads, Phone/iPad Cases and MANY other products, please visit

http://www.redbubble.com/people/coldbludd/

collections/405936-gorgeous-george

THANK YOU!

WR TING **RULES** OK

Writing Rules OK is Stuart Reid's creative writing workshop dedicated to inspiring children, young people (and teachers) to become aware of their unique power as writers, narrators and creative thinkers!

Each of the five modules looks at the specific elements of creative writing and includes exercises, classroom tools and homework sheets. The modules cover Genre, Plotting, Characters, Openers and Descriptives and these workshops can be classroom based, in small groups or as one-to-one coaching.

Writing Rules OK provides children and young adults with a basic knowledge and understanding of creative writing, with an opportunity to develop their own storytelling talents. There are several exercises included with each module, based on levels of ability, and includes Fast Finisher Extension Tasks, so whether your children are complete beginners or already becoming budding authors there's an exercise or two in each module to stretch everyone.

And there's no limit to the number of pupils or classes that can use the sessions; once you've bought each module, you can use them as often as you like. Although generally aimed at pupils between the ages of 8 and 14 years, each module lasts approx 1 hour, consisting of approx 15 minutes of audio summary and positioning, along with text-based exercises and worksheets.

www.writingrulesok.com